AN AFFAIR WITH DANGER

(NOIR NIGHTS BOOK 1)

ROBIN STOREY

DEDICATION

For Aaron

Contents

Chapter 1

When I think about the first time I laid eyes on Frankie, my mind imbues it with a significance it didn't have — a recognition of kindred souls or a premonition of a shared future. The reality was that our eyes met for a couple of seconds in a courtroom. I was intrigued by her from that moment; although I can confidently say that I made no impression on her at all. I hesitate to use the word obsession but what the hell, I already have.

And if it wasn't for my craving for a sausage roll, I wouldn't have been in that courtroom at all.

\#

June 2005

I CRANKED the car heater up and turned on the windscreen wipers against the steady drizzle. The suburban roads shone damp in the streetlights. At 10.15 on a Tuesday night, there wasn't a lot of traffic. I hated working late in winter and couldn't wait to get home to my warm, cosy apartment and collapse in front of the TV with a beer. I'd stayed back in the office to get my head around the financial reports of my newest client, a national chain of fitness centres, who'd been served with a bankruptcy notice by a creditor.

As I approached the lights of my local 7-Eleven store, I realised how hungry I was. I'd only had a sandwich at my desk for dinner. The empty parking space right in front vindicated my decision to stop. Mike was sitting behind the counter reading a newspaper.

'Hi Mike! Busy night?

Mike grinned. 'Flat out as usual. How about you?'

'Same as always. Any sausage rolls left?' I walked over to the hot food stand on the side counter. There was one sausage roll in the pie warmer. 'Must be my lucky night.'

I tore a paper bag from the hanger, took out the sausage roll and popped it into the bag. I heard the entrance buzzer beep behind me.

'Get your hands in the air!'

I whirled around. A man with a stocking over his face stood in front of the counter pointing a gun at Mike. Mike was standing, his hands raised, his face frozen into a sickly shade of pale. The man motioned to me with the gun. 'Go and stand next to him.'

I forced my legs to move. Although fear had numbed my body, my mind was in overdrive, taking in as much as it could. The man was tall and solid, and dressed in jeans, pullover and joggers. He wore a beanie and although the stocking over his face blurred his features, I could make out a broad nose and square chin.

'Is there anyone else in here?'

Mike shook his head. The man leaned forward and jabbed him in the chest with the gun. 'Don't fuck with me, mate.'

'I'm telling the truth, there's no-one else.'

The man waved his gun in the direction of the cash register. 'Empty it! And move it!'

Mike opened the register drawer. His hands shook as he pulled out the notes. The man peered out the front door, rocking back and forth on his feet.

'Hurry up!' he yelled. Mike handed him a pile of notes and the man stuffed them into his jeans pocket. He jabbed his gun into Mike's chest again. 'Is that all?'

Mike nodded. The man backed out the front door, the pistol still trained on us, then ran into the night. It was all over in less than a minute.

Chapter 2

'You're a lawyer, Mr McPherson?' Senior Detective Hunter asked.

He was an imposing man with a deliberate manner; his presence filling the small interview room at the police station.

'I'm a corporate lawyer at Chapman and Goode. I specialise in insolvency.'

'You were never tempted to do criminal law?' barked Detective Ross, a petite, dark-haired woman with an abrupt manner. Or maybe she was just having a bad day.

I shook my head. 'There's no money in criminal law, especially when you're representing the dregs of society like armed robbers.'

I neglected to mention that my father's illustrious career as a criminal law barrister before he retired to academia had also put me off, although he'd managed to make a very good living by only representing white-collar criminals.

SD Hunter pressed a button on the digital recorder on the table. 'Interview with witness William James McPherson by Senior Detective Neil Hunter and Detective Fiona Ross. Wednesday 15 June 2005 at 10 am. Mr McPherson, can you go through the events of last night again, from the moment you entered the store?'

I stared at the dewy young Queen Elizabeth 11 smiling regally at me from the painting on the wall as I recounted the events of the previous night. My heart was thumping as if it were happening all over again.

'Apart from his physical description, what else can you remember?' SD Hunter asked. 'What was his voice like?'

'Low and sort of gruff.'

'Did he have an accent?'

'He only said a few words, but he sounded Australian.'

'What about body odour?' Detective Ross asked with distaste, as if she could smell it.

'I wasn't close enough to notice, thank God.'

'Any distinguishing marks or tattoos?' she pursued.

'The only part of his body I could see were his hands and I didn't notice any marks or tattoos on them.'

SD Hunter took over again. 'What were his hands like?

'Just ordinary hands,' I snapped. 'He didn't have any fingers missing, if that's what you mean.'

He looked at me coolly.

'Sorry,' I said. 'I didn't get much sleep last night.'

After the police had arrived and taken our initial statements, I helped Mike to lock up, made sure he was okay to drive home, then drove home myself and fell into bed. I lay awake for hours, the events of the night churning over in my mind. The birds were chirping outside my window when I finally drifted off.

'What I meant, Mr McPherson, was were his hands large or small? Did he have broad fingers? Were they hairy? That sort of thing.'

I shook my head. 'Honestly, I can't remember. I was concentrating on the gun more than his hands. He seemed agitated and I was terrified the thing would go off.'

'Did he seem under the influence of alcohol or drugs?' Detective Ross asked.

'I don't think alcohol. His reflexes were too fast. Maybe drugs.'

'And you didn't see his vehicle?'

'No, I just heard a car revving up and speeding away. I was going to run outside as soon as he left to get the number plate, but Mike stopped me. He said the guy probably had an accomplice and if they saw me they could take a pot shot at me. Poor guy. It's not the first time he's been held up.'

'Thanks, that will be all,' SD Hunter said. 'If you'll wait outside, we'll get a statement typed up for you to sign.'

'There's just one thing,' I said.

SD Hunter paused. 'Yes?'

'I got the impression of strength. Not in a good way – the brutal, beat-you-till-you're-senseless kind.' I shrugged. 'I might just have imagined it because he was pointing a gun at me.'

'Thanks.' Detective Ross said. She scribbled in her notebook then looked up at me. 'How are you coping?'

'I'm fine.'

She handed me a business card. Victims of Crime Counselling Service. 'If you need support, contact this agency. You've been through a traumatic experience and sometimes the after-effects don't show up till later.'

I pocketed the card. I doubted I'd need their services. I didn't want to dwell on the experience; I wanted to put it behind me.

#

The Three Monkeys attracted a local clientele of up-and-coming professionals on a budget who appreciated cheap, hearty meals, a cosy atmosphere and music that was not only good as background noise, but that you could dance to if you were in the mood. But tonight, the crowd was more interested in watching the rugby league on the wall-sized TV or checking their iPhones than listening to me. You got those nights occasionally and after a couple of years of doing this gig every second Friday night, I didn't take it personally. It was especially hard going tonight as I hadn't slept much in the three nights since the hold-up.

I finished my set to a smattering of applause, propped my guitar on its stand and fronted up to the bar in my usual corner spot.

'Tough crowd,' Joe the bartender said, mopping up the spills in front of me.

'Yeah.'

He placed my usual order, a glass of mineral water, in front of me. I made it a rule never to drink during my gigs.

'Don't worry; you've got one fan. I'll put in an order now for your album. When are you recording it?'

'I'm still getting my song list together. It's a theme album called *Life's a Stage*, and it's about the stages of life – childhood, adolescence, adulthood, parenthood, old age and so on. I've written all the songs bar one. Every time I try, I come to a dead end.'

A large, ruddy-faced man muscled into the bar beside me. 'Two rum and cokes with ice, please.'

Joe scooped two glasses into the ice bucket. 'Let me guess which one. Parenthood?'

'No, even though I don't have kids, that song was easy. It's the one about love.'

'Ah, love,' Joe said with mock solemnity as he squirted Coke into the glasses. 'I'm no help to you. I've been married for ten years.'

'I can tell you about love, mate,' the man beside me boomed. 'You fall in love, get married, she runs off with your neighbour after 20 years, you spend the rest of your life paying out the property settlement. Write a song about that!'

'Thanks for the inspiration,' I said to his departing back.

Joe leaned forward and under the cover of the Rolling Stones blaring out 'I Can't Get No Satisfaction' from the jukebox said, 'Maybe you need a good night in the sack to stimulate your ... um ... creativity.'

I grinned. I definitely needed a good night in the sack, but wasn't so sure it would stimulate anything above my waist.

In my next set I played some covers from the 80s and 90s rather than my own stuff, but the crowd was still lukewarm. Once the football was over, it started to thin out. At 10.30, I packed up my gear and was about to load it into the car when Sarah, the assistant manager, appeared beside me.

'Would you like a drink before you go?'

I hesitated. She'd asked me the same question a couple of weeks ago and I'd given some excuse. I liked her, but I sensed she wanted more than friendship; and I wasn't sure if I wanted that with her. Statuesque blondes were not usually my thing. And I was still hurting from being dumped two months ago by Angelique, an exotic, dark-eyed brunette who'd reeled me in with curves, flounces and smoulders, and then run off with her Salsa dance teacher.

'Are you okay?' Sarah asked. 'You look a bit spaced out.'

'Yeah. I had a bit of a scary experience earlier in the week.'

I told her briefly about the hold-up. She looked aghast. 'My God, that's terrible! You should have told me before – I could have found a replacement for tonight.'

'I'm fine. Just a bit tired, so I'll pass on the drinks.'

'That's okay, I understand.'

She was disappointed, but trying not to show it. On impulse I said, 'But I'll take you up on it next time.'

She smiled. 'I'll hold you to that. Have the police caught the guy who did it?'

'Not that I'm aware of. But they will. Armed robbers are not usually known for their brains.'

Chapter 3

One year later. July 2006

An icy wind whipped around me as I stood sipping my coffee outside the front entrance of the Downing Centre District Court. Barristers hurried past me, gowns flapping and bewigged heads bent against the wind. Solicitors with briefcases and harried-looking clerks trotted after them.

A TV camera crew was setting up nearby. I wondered who the celebrity criminal was. I doubted it was Edward Gisbourne, arrested for the hold-up two weeks afterwards and held in custody since then. Armed robbers were a dime a dozen.

I downed the rest of my coffee in one gulp, trying to drown the niggle of apprehension in my gut. I had appeared in court on numerous occasions before, but in the Federal Court on behalf of clients. Never in the District Court or in the witness box.

Court was due to start in 15 minutes. I threw my coffee cup in a nearby bin and was just about to go in when I heard, 'Will!'

Mike was ambling towards me. We'd only been acquaintances before the robbery; but we'd kept in touch in the 12 months since, having the occasional drink together.

Bonded by our one common experience. He looked as if he'd slept in his shirt and his suit had obviously fitted him better when he was ten kilos lighter.

'Bastard of a day,' he said.

He reeked of stale alcohol. This was the third time he'd been the victim of a hold-up, and he'd finally accepted that working in convenience stores was not conducive to his well-being. He'd left his job and was on the dole.

'It'll be warm in the courtroom,' I said. 'Are you ready to dazzle them with your brilliant powers of observation?'

Mike grinned. 'I've been watching reruns of "Law and Order" and I know all the tricks of the trade now for outwitting the defence. Failing that, I can always break down and cry.'

'Good idea; I'll keep that in mind. Two grown men blubbering in the witness box should be enough to sway the jury.'

'We're not supposed to discussing the case,' I said in a low voice as we entered the courthouse. 'So it's best that we're not seen together, so we can't be accused of it.'

'My lips are sealed.' Mike said. We went through Security and took the lift to the fourth floor. We took our seats round the corner from courtroom two, sitting at opposite ends of the row. Our instructions were to wait there until we were called in. Despite the constant stream of people coming and going, the atmosphere was subdued, as befitted the higher status of the District Court.

The prosecutor Alex Coleby poked his head out of courtroom two, saw us sitting there and hurried over. We'd met him a couple of weeks ago at a witness briefing, to run through our evidence and give us an idea what to expect in court. He was thin and bespectacled with an intense manner, and I could well imagine him being the nerdy kid in his class at school.

He beckoned Mike over. 'I've just been advised by the defence that Gisbourne has changed his plea to guilty.'

'You're joking!' Mike said. 'The bastard decided to see sense for a change.'

'There's no altruistic motive, I can assure you,' Alex said. 'The evidence is against him and he's probably realised it and wants a discount on his sentence. Anyway, the upshot is that we don't need you, so you can go home.'

'Awesome!' Mike said. 'I'm off. Are you coming?' he asked me.

I had a pretty good idea where he was going. I had no desire to go to the pub at 9.45 in the morning.

I shook my head. 'I'm going to hang around. I want to watch him get what's coming to him.' I'd cleared my work calendar for the week in preparation for giving evidence, so I had no commitments.

Mike shrugged. 'If I never lay eyes on his ugly mug again, it will be too soon. See ya.'

I watched him as he shuffled off, feeling a pang of pity. And helplessness. Part of the reason I'd kept in touch was out of concern for his well-being. He'd refused all offers of counselling, claiming he just needed time. But meanwhile, he was drowning in alcohol. I'd had a few disturbed nights, and I hadn't gone into that 7-Eleven store since the robbery; but overall, I was coping fine.

Alex got up and nodded towards the courtroom. 'Come on in.'

I followed him into the courtroom and took a seat in the second front row near the aisle. The atmosphere was rarified and solemn, more like a church. Well, law was a religion to some. The court was about half full. I glanced casually around, wondering who the others were. Friends or relatives of the accused? Or maybe just members of the public who got a kick out of watching court cases.

I was glad that neither my brother Nick nor my sister Stephanie had accompanied me for moral support, as they'd both wanted to do. I preferred to be here on my own. Nick, an international human rights lawyer, had to fly out to a case in Egypt; but I was sure he'd only offered to come to see how many people he could impress with his credentials. Steph, who'd gone back to University to study exercise physiology after years as a physical education teacher, was in the middle of exams. My parents, though they were concerned at the time of the hold-up, still managed to convey the impression that somehow it was my fault, that I was in the wrong place at the wrong time.

Alex was in earnest conversation with the defence counsel, a man who must surely have been in his thirties but with his fresh, baby-faced complexion and startlingly blue eyes, looked barely out of high school. In his wig and gown, he looked like a teenager playing dress-ups. If he lacked experience, he had youth and ambition on his side; and he'd be keen to make his mark.

The door to the dock opened and Gisbourne entered, escorted by two police officers. It was the first time I'd seen him in the flesh since the robbery. He was taller than I remembered and broader, but it was all muscle. He wore a suit and had the sort of rough-cut look that women find attractive.

There'll be no women where you're going, mate. But he'd been in jail on remand for the last 12 months and he didn't look as if he'd suffered.

I was surprised by the heat of anger that surged inside me; I thought I'd put the robbery behind me. I wanted to wipe that smug look off his face, preferably with my fists. He sat down and I stared at him, willing him to look at me. He glanced around the courtroom, not meeting my gaze, as if he were looking for someone. His face settled into a scowl.

'All stand,' the bailiff called out. The judge entered the room and took her position at the bench. A pinch-faced woman with glasses and grey hair swept under a wig. According to the nameplate in front of her, she was Judge Delaney.

The bailiff declared the court open. Alex and the defence counsel, David Levenson, announced their appearances before the judge said, 'I believe you have some information for the court, Mr Levenson.'

'Yes, Your Honour. I have had instructions from my client this morning that he wishes to plead guilty.'

The judge glanced over at Gisbourne, still looking sulky. 'Thank you, Mr Levenson.'

She nodded to Alex, who stood up and said, 'There is an indictment before the court of two charges – one count each of armed robbery and stealing a motor vehicle. I tender it for your perusal.'

Alex handed the indictment to the judge's associate, a young female, who passed it up to her. She perused it thoroughly then handed it back to her associate. 'Please arraign the defendant.'

After a gesture from Levenson, Gisbourne stood up. The associate read the charge in a loud, clear voice. 'Edward Robert Gisbourne, you are charged that at 9.55 pm on the 5th of June 2005, you entered the 7-Eleven convenience store at 7 Makerston Street, Manly armed with a gun and committed an offence of armed robbery, stealing the approximate sum of $750. How do you plead?

'Guilty.'

I heard the whish of the courtroom door opening. Gisbourne looked over and his expression changed instantly into a wide grin. I looked around.

A woman had entered. Tall, a mass of wild reddish-auburn hair that appeared to be exploding from her head. Startling red lips, too much eye make-up. She sashayed down the aisle on her high heels, her jeans and purple breast-hugging top under a denim jacket clinging to her as if they'd been painted on. Skinny except in the chest department.

It seemed as if the whole courtroom was holding its breath watching her. She stared straight ahead with an expression that said, 'I know you're all watching me and I don't give a damn.'

She stopped at my row. 'Excuse me.'

I drew my legs in. As she brushed past me, I caught a whiff of her perfume. Musky. She sat at the opposite end of the row near the wall, dumping her bright pink handbag on the floor and crossing her legs. Shiny crimson toenails peeked out from her open-toed sandals. Gisbourne mouthed, 'love you,' to her and she blew him a kiss back.

'Edward Robert Gisbourne, you are charged that at...' The judge's associate read the second charge. Judge Delaney stared at the new arrival with knitted brow and tight lips; but she was looking at her boyfriend, oblivious or uncaring. I guessed the latter.

How many times had she sat in a courtroom looking at him in the dock? I had no knowledge of Gisbourne's history but I was pretty sure this wasn't his first offence. He had the demeanour of a career criminal. What sort of a woman would knowingly hang around with an armed robber? One who had form herself, obviously. Surely no law-abiding woman would choose to be in a relationship with him.

After Gisbourne had pleaded guilty, the judge looked over the top of her glasses at Alex. 'Mr Coleby, do you require an adjournment so that you and Mr Levenson can prepare the facts for sentence?'

Alex stood up. 'Yes, Your Honour, a month will be adequate.'

'Sentencing is adjourned for a month on a date to be fixed. Is there an application for bail, Mr Levenson?'

'No, Your Honour.'

We all stood, the judge swept out and the bailiff declared the court closed.

As the police officers escorted Gisbourne out of the dock, he mouthed, 'love you,' again to his girlfriend before disappearing. I couldn't help glancing across at her to see her reaction. She grinned at him and waved. Then, catching my eye, her expression changed instantly, its meaning clear. *What's it to you?* I quickly looked away.

As we filed out of the courtroom, she brushed past me and squeezed into the lift just as the door was closing. I took the next lift; and as I exited the courthouse, I spotted her trotting along the sidewalk. I watched the provocative sway of her hips and arse, wondering if she always walked like that, or if it was just the heels.

The wind had died down but the coldness hung in the air like a thick blanket. She fumbled in her bag, took out a packet of cigarettes and a lighter and lit a cigarette, not missing a stride.

Chapter 4

One month later. August 2006.

I arrived at Court an hour early and sat outside the courtroom working on my latest case on my iPad. Partly out of need, but also to distract myself. The prospect of spending another day staring at the perpetrator of the crime against me was not one I relished, but I wanted to see justice done.

Something made me look up. Gisbourne's girlfriend was heading towards me. Mini-dress, jacket, purple tights, boots. Bangles jostling up each arm. Same uncontrollable hair and defiant expression. People stared. She had presence. Boho no-bullshit-chick presence.

She made straight for the courtroom, wrenched open the door and went in. I checked my watch. Court was due to start in 10 minutes. I packed my iPad into my briefcase and entered the courtroom. She was sitting in the second row against the wall, the same place as last time. As if it was her designated seat. She took a mobile phone out of her handbag and began to scroll down the screen.

Both barristers were already at the bar table. There were plenty of empty seats but on an impulse I sat in her row, at a respectable distance. That same perfume wafted over. She looked up from her phone and I took my chance.

'Hi, how are you?'

To this day, I don't know what made me do it. I'm not the sort that strikes up conversation with strange women, but something about her compelled me to do it.

She stared at me. Her eyes were the deepest brown. Alive, intense. 'Do I know you?'

'No. I'm Will.' Awkward silence. 'I just wondered ... this must be difficult for you.'

Her eyes narrowed. 'Are you a reporter?'

'No, just an interested party.'

'Oh, I get it. Just here for the fun of it.'

'I don't think anyone here would call it fun. Except maybe the barristers.'

'So what's your interest?'

'I was in the 7-Eleven store when your boyfriend held it up.'

I watched her expression as my reply sank in. There were no discernible signs of empathy, but I sensed it was there. In the subtle change of her body posture.

'So you're here to see him get his just desserts?'

'You got it. Wouldn't you do the same thing if you were in my shoes?'

She didn't answer. At that moment, Gisbourne was led into the dock. He glanced over at his girlfriend, whose name, I realised, I still didn't know, but he refrained from any mimed declarations of love. His barrister had probably had a word to him – it wasn't the sort of behaviour that endeared the accused to the court. His more subdued air did little to diminish his aura of cocky bravado.

The girl smiled and waved, and slid her mobile phone back in her bag just as Judge Delaney entered the courtroom.

First on the agenda was the prosecutor's submission. Alex Coleby's speech was clear and to the point, the essence of it being that the offence was not a spur-of-the-moment occurrence, but had been planned and cold-bloodedly executed.

'The defendant at some unknown time obtained an illegal firearm and on the morning of the offence he stole a car,' he said in his clear, high voice. 'He changed the number plates and that night went to the 7-Eleven convenience store at Manly, on the other side of the city from where he lived, and threatened the occupants of the store with no regard for the consequences to them. And furthermore, he admitted to being under the influence of methamphetamine at the time of the offence, and that he was addicted to this drug.'

I watched Gisbourne's face. He stared impassively at the floor in front of him, as if what the prosecutor was saying had nothing to do with him. *Look at me, you cowardly bastard!*

His girlfriend shifted several times in her seat. Maybe sitting next to the victim of her boyfriend's crime was making her uncomfortable. I hoped so.

Alex summed up. 'With regards to sentencing, I acknowledge the offender's early plea, which has saved the time and expense of a trial; however, that is all I can say in his favour. He was verbally abusive towards police when initially arrested and only calmed down when threatened with further charges. He was also subsequently uncooperative with police, refusing to disclose the identity of his co-offender, the driver of the stolen car, who, I understand, still remains at large. He also refused to disclose how and where he obtained the weapon used in the offence, which has not been recovered.

'Furthermore, the defendant has history for a like offence in Western Australia eight years ago, in 1998. In this state, while he has no previous like offences, it is noted that he committed one offence of common assault in 2004 and two offences of breach of domestic violence order in 2002 and 2004. Both of these offences contain elements of physical violence towards the aggrieved. Here is a man, drug addiction or not, for whom violence is normal behaviour and over which he clearly has no control. Such a man is a danger to the community and if this behaviour continues to escalate, there will continue to be victims, and quite possibly more serious consequences. I submit that the defendant should be given a sentence that reflects the severity of the offence and that will also act as a deterrence against future like behaviour. Your Honour, I refer to the case of...

He went on at length about a couple of precedents. I darted a sideways glance at his girlfriend. Was she the aggrieved in the domestic violence offences? Despite her slight build, she gave the impression she could give as good as she got, though she'd be no match for someone like Gisbourne.

Alex's final recommendation was six years imprisonment, with a non-parole period of two years for the armed robbery and three months imprisonment for stealing a motor vehicle. Gisbourne glanced over at the girl. His face was set, his mouth tight. I continued staring at him and finally his eyes met mine, lingering for a fraction of a second before moving away. But I knew he'd recognised me. I was triumphant that I'd forced him to acknowledge my presence. It went a little way towards diffusing my hostility.

David Levenson rose to present his submission. 'Your Honour, I acknowledge, as my friend has said, that the offence does appear to have been cold-blooded and premeditated, with no thought for the consequences or the effect on the victims. I'd like to, if I may, apprise you of the other side of the story, because there is, of course, always another side to the story – sometimes several.'

Levenson's tone of voice, belying his fresh-faced appearance, was warm and persuasive. Born to his profession. That or politics.

'Your Honour, the defendant is a 32-year-old man, who like many others who've committed such crimes, comes from an unfortunate background. His father left the family when the defendant was two years old, leaving his mother to bring him and his two older brothers up by herself. She had her own issues, being an abuser of prescription drugs, and had a series of relationships with men of less than desirable character, many of whom were violent alcoholics. As a consequence, the defendant was subjected to constant physical and emotional abuse from a very young age. He started using drugs, namely cannabis, at the age of 12 as a way of coping with this abuse, and left home at 14 after being assaulted by his mother's partner. He was living on the streets for a couple of years and that's when he started using methamphetamines, the cause of the offence in respect of which he has pleaded guilty today.

'Due to his drug use his employment history has been sporadic, but the positions he has held have required some degree of skill and responsibility. He has worked as a salesman for various companies, a warehouse supervisor and a foreman for a construction company. He's been drug-free for the last 12 months while on remand in custody and consequently has been able to think clearly for the first time in years. He's very remorseful for his actions and particularly for the effect they have had on the two victims.'

Yeah, right. Remorse for getting caught. And the old, crappy upbringing chestnut. His childhood was horrific, but I couldn't feel any sympathy for him. If it hadn't been me and Mike he'd held up, maybe. But then again, probably not. Both Mike and I had been asked if we wanted to submit a victim impact statement to the court, but we both declined. Neither of us felt a burning need to do it and surmised that it would make little impact on Gisbourne.

'The defendant instructs that on the morning of the offence, he'd been to a job interview in Parramatta and was about to catch the train home when he saw a car on the side of the road with the window down. On an impulse he decided to steal it, thinking that it would it be a lot easier to get a job if he had a car. He admits to changing the plates to avoid being apprehended but denies that he stole the car specifically to commit the armed robbery. At that stage, he instructs, the idea hadn't even occurred to him.

'That night, he had a fight with his girlfriend, with whom he resides, because they'd run out of money to buy food. She hadn't had any work for a couple of weeks and his unemployment benefits had been stopped due to a mix-up; and so they had no money to obtain food for dinner. He instructs he decided to go out and hold up the store to get money for food and that it was indeed a spur-of-the-moment offence. He denies obtaining the weapon in order to commit the offence and that he had previously purchased it for self-defence, having been threatened by an acquaintance over a longstanding grudge.

'He also freely admits to being under the influence of methamphetamine at the time he made this decision, which he realises is no excuse of course; but he also instructs that he would not have entertained the thought of committing an armed robbery if he hadn't been under the influence of drugs. He admits it was a very foolish decision with no regard for the consequences for himself or the victims. Drug addiction is essentially a very selfish affliction; the addict cannot and does not think about anything or anyone except himself and getting his next fix, and the defendant has been a user of drugs since he was 12, so that's some 20 years. As I mentioned before, he's had plenty of thinking time in custody to ponder the effects of his actions.

'I've had conversations with the defendant, Your Honour, about not only the psychological and emotional trauma the victims have undoubtedly suffered, but also the effect on wider society. Convenience stores that are open late at night are sitting targets for offences of this kind, and customers get to the stage where they are too scared to go in at night for fear that the same thing will happen to them. Thus resulting in loss of revenue for the store owner. The defendant has admitted that he has never considered these factors before and that it's been a big eye-opener for him. Consequently, as I mentioned earlier, he has displayed considerable remorse for his actions.'

If that was true, he was hiding it remarkably well. Unexciting as my job was, I was glad for the umpteenth time I hadn't followed my father's wishes and gone into criminal law, that I didn't have to get up in court and spout things I knew were utter bullshit.

The barrister paused for a few seconds, ostensibly to look through his notes, but really to give the judge time to fully appreciate his client's remorse.

'Your Honour, the defendant has been in a relationship for the past seven years with Francis Slater, who is present here today.'

There was a rustle of movement as people in the courtroom looked around. Gisbourne gave his girlfriend a subdued grin.

'Ms Slater is 25 and works as a cleaner. She and the defendant have been together for seven years; they're in a stable relationship; and the defendant has realised that at the age of 32, it's about time he cleaned up his act, gained employment and became a productive member of society. One point in his favour is that he has had periods of abstinence from drugs for up to 2 years, when he's held down jobs and stayed out of trouble so he's more than capable of doing so when he puts his mind to it. He and Ms Slater plan to have a family and he's realised the life he's been leading is not conducive to responsible fatherhood, and indeed he wants his own children to have the stable and happy childhood that he himself was unfortunate enough not to have.

'With regard to sentencing, Your Honour, I ask that you take into account the defendant's decision to change his plea to guilty, thus averting the cost and time of a trial by jury. And while I'm not at all making light of the effect of the offence on the victims, I'd also ask Your Honour to consider that although violence was threatened, none was actually carried out. I acknowledge his history of recent violence, in the charges of assault and breach of domestic violence order, but it is noted that his previous offence of armed robbery was committed eight years ago and there have been no serious violent offences since then.

'The sentencing range for an offence of this nature ranges from four to eight years, and taking into account the circumstances mentioned, I respectfully request that you consider imposing the minimum penalty of four years, with parole eligibility after serving a third of that sentence, that is 16 months imprisonment. I submit that the defendant's prospects for rehabilitation are good, especially if subjected to parole supervision upon release; and he has indicated a willingness to attend drug counselling and any other intervention considered necessary as part of his parole.'

He bowed his head. 'That is my submission, Your Honour, if I can be of any further assistance...'

'Thank you Mr Levenson. I need further time to consider sentencing, so I'll adjourn the court until 2 pm.'

We all filed out, except for Francis, as I now knew her, who brushed past me with an impatient 'excuse me' and bolted out the door.

#

There were three hours to kill. The day was cold and damp, like walking into a wet sponge. The responsible thing to do would be to find a cafe and work over an early lunch. Plus I had a few missed calls from the office. Francis stood a little way ahead of me on the sidewalk, fumbling in her handbag, a cigarette perched between her lips – neon pink lips that you could see in the dark. I wasn't going to do the responsible thing.

She looked up as I approached. 'Hey mate, have you got a light?'

'Sorry, I don't smoke.' I scouted the crowds bustling past. 'But I'll find you one, if you like.'

Further down the sidewalk, a middle-aged man in a suit was standing off to the side, puffing on a cigarette while checking his phone. I approached him and asked him for a light.

'It's not for me, it's for the lady over there,' I said, though why I should care if a perfect stranger thought I was a smoker, I had no idea.

He followed my gaze to where Francis was standing, her auburn hair shining even on this dull day. He handed me his lighter. 'Tell her she can have it, my compliments,' he said.

'The gentleman said you could keep it,' I said, as I handed her the lighter.

'Really? Thanks.' She lit her cigarette and drew in a deep lungful. 'I'd given up before this.' She inclined her head in the direction of the courthouse.

'It must be very stressful for you,' I said.

She shrugged. 'I'm kinda used to it.'

'I'm going to have a coffee. Would you like to come?'

She gave me a speculative look, then turned her head away to blow out a cloud of smoke. 'Thanks, but no thanks.'

'Are you sure? My shout.'

'Yes, I am sure and I'm perfectly capable of buying my own coffee if I wanted one.'

She drew out her mobile phone from her bag. 'I've got some calls to make.'

'Okay, see you later, Francis.'

She gave me a sharp look. 'I hate that name. It's Frankie.'

'Suits you. See you, Frankie.'

Chapter 5

I was already back in court, in the same seat, when Frankie walked in. She sat in the row behind me. A deliberate snub. Did she think my asking her for coffee was a pick-up line? It wasn't meant to be; I'd never been good at chatting up women. I always liked to see if we had anything in common before I started honing in. What was it then, if it wasn't a pick-up line? It was obvious that Frankie and I would have little, if anything, in common.

The court resumed and Judge Delaney began her sentencing remarks in her dry, precise voice. She outlined the facts of the case and the information taken into account in her sentence. Gisbourne stood with his gaze fixed upon a spot somewhere above her head.

I was acutely aware of Frankie's presence behind me. What must it be like, sitting in a courtroom watching your partner being sentenced to prison and knowing he'd be locked away for who knows how long? Long, lonely days and nights. The nights would be the worst. It was her own fault, anyway. What was the saying? If you run with wolves you'll learn how to howl.

The judge paused to give Gisbourne a long look, and I knew then that she hadn't been swayed by Levenson's arguments. 'Unfortunately, armed robbery is becoming more common with the rise in use of methamphetamines, with serious consequences for the victims and the community at large. It is to be hoped, Mr Gisbourne, that you take Mr Levenson's advice and think about your future while you're in custody. In respect of the offence of armed robbery, you're sentenced to six years imprisonment, with a non-parole period of two years. In respect of the offence of stealing a motor vehicle, I sentence you to three months imprisonment, to be served concurrently. I also take into account your pre-sentence custody of thirteen months, one week and three days.'

Gisbourne's demeanour was of a man who knew he was beaten, but he was damned if he was going to show it. The sentence wasn't as bad as I'd thought. With the pre-sentence custody discount and if he were granted parole after two years, he'd serve less than 12 months behind bars.

'Anything further, Mr Coleby? Mr Levenson?' the judge asked.

'No, Your Honour,' they both said.

Gisbourne mouthed a defiant 'love you' in Frankie's direction before the police officers led him out of the dock. I restrained myself from looking around to see her reaction. The court was dismissed and she strode out of the courtroom ahead of me.

Outside it was just starting to drizzle. Drizzle that meant business. Pedestrians quickened their pace, umbrellas snapped up. Frankie was almost out of view.

'Frankie!' I shouted. She stopped, looked around and watched me dodging people and umbrellas as I sprinted towards her.

'What the fuck do you want?'

One tear was running down her cheek and she swiped at it.

'I just wanted to say…' What did I want to say? I pulled out my wallet and took out a business card.

'Here's my card. If you need help with … I dunno, anything, just call me.'

She took the card. 'A fucking lawyer. I should have known. And why the hell do you think I'd need an insolvency lawyer?'

'I take on other cases as well. That's just my specialty.'

Her look could have cut glass. 'If you're thinking you'll get a bit of action because my boyfriend's in prison, you can fuck off.'

'Hey, it's not…'

'Or is this some weird revenge fantasy because he held you up?'

'Neither. I have no ulterior motives. If you don't want to take my card, that's fine.'

'I've never met a man without ulterior motives.'

But she pocketed my card and strode off. I watched her as she disappeared into the crowd. It was only then that I realised the drizzle had become a downpour and I was getting drenched.

Chapter 6

At the Three Monkeys, I played my heart out and the crowd responded, cheering and whistling. I played all the popular covers from the Rolling Stones to the Black Keys and soon the dance floor was packed.

During my break, I got my mineral water from Joe and joined Sarah at a corner table.

'You're on fire tonight,' she smiled.

'I think it's the relief from the court case being over. And not having to give evidence.'

'I'm glad for your sake it's over. How's your album coming along?'

'It's not.' I'd mentally kicked myself many times for telling Joe and Sarah about my album. Every time they asked me about it, it reminded me that I'd made zilch progress over the last 12 months. I'd lost the momentum on my songwriting and couldn't motivate myself to get back into it.

'I've got writer's block,' I said. It was as good an excuse as any.

'I've got a friend who's a writer and she says writers' block is really fear in disguise.' She put her hand on mine. 'I think you should keep at it. I really like your songs.'

I was uncomfortable with the hand bit. We'd had the occasional after-gig drink, and Sarah had thrown out a few hints about us going out on a date. I told her as tactfully as I could that I liked her as a friend but nothing more. And it was true. She was hurt at first and things were uncomfortable between us for a while, but it blew over and we were back to being friends again.

But every now and then, she would initiate some physical contact, perhaps testing the waters to see if I'd changed my mind. If I were like some of my mates, I would have taken up her invitation for the sake of regular sex, but I didn't want to take advantage of her. Particularly as she did all the hiring and firing of staff for the hotel, so technically she was my boss. Screwing the boss is never a good thing.

'Thanks.' I stood up. 'I guess I'd better get back to it. My fans are screaming for me.'

#

My lungs were bursting and my legs were screaming 'Stop!' I forced myself to keep going, pounding away my tiredness on the treadmill at the gym. I hadn't slept well since the sentencing two weeks ago, waking up exhausted after vivid dreams that disappeared from my memory as soon as I opened my eyes. During the day, images of Frankie haunted me – her hair, her eyes, her smoky-jazz-club voice, her feistiness. I wanted to know more about her, her life and how she came to be the girlfriend of an armed robber. The frustrating thing was I had no idea why I had this obsession.

After eventually giving in to my legs, I showered at the gym and drove home, picking up a take-away curry on the way. My surge of energy from the jogging quickly dissipated under the influence of a couple of beers and the Massaman curry. I turned on the TV, sank into my couch and tried to work out in a logical, rational way what attracted me to Frankie. But there was nothing I could put into words.

The evidence against my seeing her again was overwhelming. She was in a relationship with a criminal, she and I were planets apart in every respect, and we'd have nothing in common. And she already thought I was a jerk. What was the evidence in favour? None. She had my business card, but the chances of her contacting me were practically non-existent. Did I want to sleep with her? Hell, yeah. That was the weirdest part. She was so unlike any woman I'd ever been attracted to before. When I weighed it all up, I decided it was lust, pure and simple. It had been a while since I'd got my rocks off.

I got up and retrieved my iPad from my briefcase. If I researched her on the internet and found out as much about her as I could, it would satisfy my curiosity and I could stop thinking about her. I started with Facebook. There were plenty of people called Francis Slater, but the only one that fitted had a one-line entry – 'Lives in Sydney, Australia' – with no photo. When I clicked on the link, a message popped up saying that her profile was only visible to people she knew. That made sense – the police checked Facebook, it was one of their main sources of information, and if your partner was a criminal, you'd hardly want the police sniffing around your Facebook pages. I declined Facebook's invitation to send her a friend request. I had an inkling it wouldn't be well received.

I then googled Francis Slater and came up with Dr Francis Slater from Cambridge University chairing an economics conference, Francis Slater, a devout elder of the Springfield Uniting Church who was sorely missed after her untimely death and Francis Slater the would-be American Idol, caterwauling her rendition of 'I Will Always Love You' on YouTube.

Google also informed me that there were eight Francis Slaters on LinkedIn. As this was a social media network for business people, I doubted she'd be there; but I checked each profile just in case. I couldn't find any newspaper or TV reports about her and I even searched Pinterest, because of its high proportion of female users. Nothing.

What now? It would be easy enough to find out where she lived. The court and the prison would both have her address listed as Gisbourne's next of kin. I had a mate, Jerry, who was a criminal lawyer – it would be easy enough to get that information through him. But that was unethical. Not to mention getting into creepy, stalker territory.

Forget her. She's trouble with a capital T.

Chapter 7

'I'm sorry, Mrs McNamara, but I can't help you regarding your husband's alleged offshore accounts. You'll need to see a forensic accountant...'

Mrs McNamara was too wound up to listen. I held the phone away from my ear as she continued her rant about my client, her rotten-to-the-core ex-husband who, according to her, was claiming bankruptcy to avoid paying his share of their property settlement, when she knew for a fact that he had millions stashed away in an overseas account.

'I really have to go, Mrs McNamara, I have a client waiting. Take my advice and hire an accountant.'

I hung up and hardly had time to breathe a sigh of relief when my mobile phone rang. Unknown number.

'Hi, it's Frankie.'

I sat motionless with shock. My heart skipped a couple of beats. 'Hi, how are you?'

'Okay.' A pause. 'You told me I could call you if I needed help.'

'Absolutely. What can I do for you?'

'I'd prefer to talk in person. Have you got time today?'

I checked my diary. I was just about to go to an in-house seminar on bankruptcy law changes, and I had meetings with clients for the rest of the day.

'Sure. Do you want to meet for coffee somewhere?'

'I haven't got time. I'm at work, at the Ocean Waves Resort at Bondi. I get half an hour for lunch at 12. Can you meet me in the foyer?"

'No worries, I'll be there.'

I knocked on the office door of my boss, Louis, the partner in charge of the insolvency team. He worked hard and played hard and expected his team to do the same.

'I've got a killer migraine. I need to go home and lie down in a dark room.'

Louis gave me a searching look. 'Stress not getting to you, is it?'

'No, it's just appeared out of nowhere.' I swallowed my guilt. 'Sorry about the seminar. I'll get the info later and I'll ask Chloe to reschedule this afternoon's appointments.'

#

I took my briefcase with me, not sure if this was a professional or personal matter. It was a 30-minute drive from my office in Surry Hills to Bondi and I arrived there half an hour early. I had a coffee at one of the beachfront cafes then drove to the Ocean Waves Resort. It was a red brick three-storey building one block back from the beach, obviously well past its prime. Beach towels hung over peeling balcony railings. A battered campervan straddled the two guest carpark spaces.

I parked on the street and entered the foyer at two minutes to twelve. An odour of grease and wet towels hung in the air. The reception desk was unattended. A woman grasping the hand of a screaming toddler waited by the lift. The door slid open and Frankie bowled out. The woman hauled the child in and its screams echoed inside the lift as the door closed and the lift creaked on its way.

'Thanks for coming at such short notice,' Frankie said. She wore a tabard over her jeans inscribed with the words 'Mrs Magic Cleaning', her neon pink handbag slung over her shoulder. Somehow she'd managed to tame her hair into a bundle under a cap, from which strands hung down and curled around her face. She was the only woman I'd met who could look stunning in cleaning attire.

'That's okay. I didn't have much on. Do you want to go and grab a sandwich?'

'Thanks but I don't have time. There's a seat out the back.'

I followed her through a door at the back of the foyer, which led into a small garden courtyard with a couple of bench seats. Another girl in jeans and tabard got up and left, texting on her phone as she went. We sat down in the warm sun and Frankie lit a cigarette. I instinctively leaned away. I hate the smell of cigarette smoke and one of my non-negotiable criteria for dates was that they had to be a non-smoker. I'd never even kissed a smoker, let alone gone to bed with one.

'Sorry,' Frankie said, moving her cigarette away from me. 'I've been meaning to give up but it hasn't happened yet.'

She crossed her legs, her foot jiggling madly. Her nerviness was palpable. I longed to touch her arm to reassure her.

'You seem a bit on edge,' I said.

'I'm fine. The reason I wanted to see you was to ask you if you could help me find my brother.'

I don't know what I was expecting, but it certainly wasn't that.

'What's the story? Is he a missing person?'

She dug into her jeans pocket, pulled out a small wallet and from it produced a crumpled photo. It was of a boy and a girl aged, I guessed, around seven and five. The boy was sitting in the girl's lap, her arms around him. The girl's brown, auburn-tinged hair sprouted from the side of her head in two pigtails and the boy's hair was pure snow-blonde. His cheeky grin suffused his entire face, tilted slightly upwards as if acknowledging the protective presence of the girl behind him. The girl was smiling but there was a sadness and resignation in her eyes that I'd rarely, if ever, seen in such a young face.

'That's me and him. I was six and he was four. His name's Jacob Van Graf. He's my half-brother. This was taken just before we both went into foster care – it's the only one I have of him.'

I waited while she took a drag of her cigarette. 'We both went to different foster parents even though they're supposed to keep siblings together. They also promised me I'd be able to see him, but that didn't happen either.'

Her voice was hard with bitterness. She stared at the photo. 'I haven't seen him since they took him away. I've tried to find him and all I know is that the foster family he went to when he was 10 adopted him when he was 12. And because they don't want their details given out, I can't find out anything more. I've spent a fortune putting public notices in newspapers asking him to contact me or anyone who knows him. For all I know, he could have changed his name.'

'Isn't there an agency you can register with if you're looking for a family member who's been adopted?'

'Yes, the Reunion and Information Register. I've registered with them, but Jake hasn't. They can only help you if both parties are on it.'

She leaned over and stubbed her cigarette out forcefully on the rock border of the garden. 'So I just wondered, with you being a lawyer, whether you'd be able to track him down. I'm not good with people in government departments – they just piss me off and I end up swearing at them.'

'If the foster family don't want their details disclosed, it will be difficult to track him down. But I can give it a go. I'll need you to sign a form authorising me to get information on your behalf. Even then, the authorities may not tell me anything. Have you got an email address?'

She nodded. I took a pen and notebook out of my briefcase and handed it to her. 'Write it down, as well as your phone number. And your brother's name and date of birth, and your address before he went into the foster home. Do you know the name of the foster family he went to or where they lived?'

She shook her head. 'They tell you nothing; you're just another kid to them. I didn't even know we were going to be separated until the child safety officers came to the house to take him to his foster family. When they told me I wasn't going with him, I screamed and tried to drag Jake away from them; and then I tried to get in the car with them. One of them had to stay behind with me to try and calm me down, but I refused to.'

She took the pen and started writing.

'So why were you both put in a foster home? Where were your parents?'

'My father left when I was a baby. Mum's partner, Jake's dad, left her for another woman. She started drinking again and couldn't look after us. We didn't have any other family.'

'Give me the names and dates of birth of your mother and Jake's father as well. The more information I have, the better.'

She finished writing, gave me back the notebook, then dug into her handbag and handed me a crumpled sheet of paper. 'This is my Adoption Information Certificate, which says I've got the right to search for information about Jake.'

She gave me a sideways glance. 'I appreciate you doing this. I can't afford to pay you.'

'I don't expect you to. Consider yourself my pro bono project for the year. Just have a coffee with me occasionally, that's all I ask."

Stony silence.

'Purely as your legal advisor of course.'

'I can't meet you for coffee. If we have to meet, we can do it in my lunch hour. If that suits you,' she added grudgingly.

She looked at her watch and sprang to her feet. 'I gotta go.'

I took hold of her arm. She tried to wrench it away, but I kept a firm hold. 'Frankie, I'm more than happy to help you, and if you want to meet in your lunch hour, that's fine. But I want you to be straight with me. Why are you so jumpy? Who or what are you afraid of?'

She stared at a point somewhere over my shoulder. 'If Eddie finds out I've been talking to you, he'll send someone around to beat me up. And you.'

'Why? Doesn't he want you to find your brother?'

'It's got nothing to do with that. He doesn't want me to have anything to do with other men while he's in jail.'

'That's ridiculous! How's he going to know?'

'He has lots of mates on the outside; they report back to him.'

'So his mates are following your every move? That sounds like bullshit to me.'

'You don't know him; you don't know what he's capable of.'

Then, obviously remembering my part in the hold-up, she added, 'In a relationship, I mean.'

On the one hand, I wanted to say,' Tell me then. What does he do to you?' And another part of me didn't want to know.

'I'll let you get back to work,' I said. 'I'll email you the authority form; and after you sign it and email it back to me, I'll get started.'

Chapter 8

Frankie emailed me the signed authority form the next day. In my lunch hour at work, over my salad wrap, I studied the information she'd given me. Jacob Mitchell Van Graf DOB 6 June 1983. Frances Margaret Slater DOB 23 March 1981. That made Jacob 23, two years younger than Frankie. Address 64 Bryants Rd Macquarie Fields. Mother Adele Pauline Hoffman DOB 13 July 1959. Father of Jacob, Thomas Witton. Frankie didn't know his second name or date of birth.

It took two weeks of phone calls and emails to Family and Community Services to obtain any information. I came to the same roadblock that Frankie had. Jacob had lived with a number of different foster families before being taken in by a foster family at the age of 10, who officially adopted him when he was 12. They requested that their details not be disclosed to anyone outside the department; and despite my turning on all the charm I could muster, the clerk refused to divulge if Jacob had changed his name upon adoption, or even the town he'd lived in.

There was nothing for it but to play my one and only trump card. I called Family and Community Services again and made sure I was talking to a female clerk I hadn't spoken to before. I figured a woman was more likely to respond to my tactic. I told her the whole story of my search and explained my predicament.

'I know you have your confidentiality policy and I respect that. Normally I wouldn't even think of asking you this, but these are special circumstances. Ms Slater is ill with cancer and the doctors have given her six months maximum. And the only thing she wants to do before she dies is to find her brother. Now, as I'm sure you know, the doctors can only guess when it comes to cancer – she might live for two years or she may only last two months, so time is of the essence. She realises that Jake, for whatever reason, may not want anything to do with her; but she's prepared for that. She just wants to find him and know he's okay, so she can die in peace.'

Silence.

'I can email you a doctor's certificate if you like, verifying her illness.'

Please don't say yes.

The clerk, who'd identified herself as Leslie, gave a deep sigh. 'What I can do is phone the foster parents myself and ask them if they're prepared to talk to you. If they are, I can pass on your contact details; then it's up to them.'

'That would be much appreciated.'

Leslie called back two days later. 'I tried to contact the family, but both the home and mobile numbers have been disconnected. It's been a while since we've had contact with them, so they've either changed their phone numbers or moved house. There's really nothing more I can do.'

It was obvious I'd already stretched our friendship to its limits. But I had to give it one last try.

'I appreciate your help and I don't want to take up any more of your time, so I'm wondering if you could do one last thing for me – for Frankie. Could you tell me the town Jacob was living in with his adoptive family?'

'I'm sorry, I can't do that.'

'It would be an enormous help. Otherwise we have no idea where to start searching and time is running out for Frankie.'

'Mr McPherson, you know as well as I do that I'd be breaching confidentiality to disclose that information. I can't help you any further.'

She hung up. I stared at the overflowing in-tray on my desk. There had to be a way. I was still mulling over it when my phone rang twenty minutes later. An unknown mobile number.

'Mr McPherson, it's Lesley from Family and Community Services. I'm ringing you from my personal mobile phone – our conversations on the department line are recorded.'

She paused then said in a rush, 'I can tell you the name of the town Jacob was living in, but please don't tell anyone that I told you, not even Ms Slater. I'd get fired if anyone found out.'

'Thanks, Leslie, I appreciate it and you have my word that I'll tell no-one, including Frankie.'

'He was living in Gosford. That's all I can tell you.'

I thanked her, hung up and did a fist pump in the air. But when I came down from my high, I reminded myself there was still a lot I didn't know. In my lunch hour, I took a cab to the electoral office in Haymarket (easier than driving there and trying to find a parking space) and searched in all states for Jacob van Graf. Nothing. Which meant he'd changed his name, had never registered for voting or was living in another country.

#

When I got back to the office, I rang Frankie. She answered straight away.

'I've made some progress. I've found out that Jake was living in Gosford.'

'Fucking fantastic! Whereabouts in Gosford?'

'They wouldn't give me the address. I had to lie through my teeth to get that much information.'

'How are we going to find him? That's if he's even still living there.'

'That's the million dollar question. He may not still be living with his family; but at least if we can find them, they'll know where he is.'

'I'll have to go to Gosford and see if I can find anyone who knows him.'

'The other complication is that the family may no longer be in Gosford either.' I told her about Leslie's attempts to phone Jacob's family.

'But it's a start, isn't it?' Frankie said. 'If we can find out where he used to live, someone might know where he's gone.'

'It's a slim hope, but it's all we've got,' I agreed.

'That settles it. I'm definitely going to Gosford. The boss probably won't give me leave, so I'll have to quit my job.'

'Don't quit your job. Not yet. I'll do some more digging around, see what I can find.'

'Thanks. I appreciate you doing this.'

After dinner I sat on my deck with a beer and a notebook and pen, brainstorming further ideas for tracking down Jacob. Below me on the road, the car lights winked through the Norfolk pines. The rhythmic crash of the surf was clear in the night air, the fresh breeze carrying its salty tang. The ocean views were the main reason I'd bought the apartment at Coogee Beach and I never tired of the sound and smell of the sea.

Gosford was a city with a population of over 160,000. To find someone who had lived there but may not live there any more, and who may well have changed his name was a challenge, to say the least. By the end of the night I had three items on my list. Schools, sporting clubs and police check.

Chapter 9

My search results were disheartening. I phoned every primary and secondary school in Gosford asking if they'd had a student named Jacob van Graf who may have changed his surname at 12. But of course they told me nothing and my signed authority form didn't impress them at all. The same with the sporting clubs. As I was not a criminal lawyer, an enquiry for a police check would arouse suspicions, so I asked my criminal lawyer mate Jerry to do a criminal history check for Jacob, on the off-chance he could be traced through the courts or was in jail.

'What's this for?' Jerry asked.

'Just helping out a friend.'

'Female, by any chance?'

'Yes, but not that sort of friend.'

'Why not? You're not still upset about Angela, are you? That was ages ago.'

'Angelique. And no, I'm not still upset about her. Unlike you, I'm picky about the women I go out with. I prefer someone who can string a few words together without giggling and thrusting her cleavage at me.'

'Your standards are way too high, mate.'

Jerry phoned back a couple of hours later. 'Sorry, nothing on Mr van Graf. Gotta go. I'm due back in court. I'll invite you and your girlfriend who's not a girlfriend over for a barbecue soon.'

What now? This exercise was turning into a maze, full of dead ends. I thought back over the calls I'd made to the schools in Gosford. There was one to Northwoods State Secondary College. I'd spoken to the principal's personal assistant, a youngish-sounding woman named Amanda. She gave me the usual spiel about not being able to divulge information and when I played my trump card about Frankie's terminal cancer, she hesitated as if about to say something, then said hurriedly, 'I'm really sorry about your client's illness, but unfortunately I still can't give out that information.'

Her momentary hesitation made me think that she'd recognised the name. If Jacob had stayed at high school until Year 12, he would have left only 6 years ago. If she'd been working at the school back then, she'd more than likely remember him. His unusual name and circumstances, as a child in a foster/adoptive family would have set him apart from the rest of the students. It was a long shot but our only lead. And the only way to get any further was to front up to the school in person.

#

As Frankie was doing an early shift, I arranged to meet her at 3.30 after work.

'Will you be back this afternoon?' Chloe asked me as I headed out the door.

'Probably not.'

From the look she gave me, I knew what she was thinking. *You're up to something and it involves a woman.*

Frankie was working at Bondi again but at a different resort – a glittering oceanfront high-rise. She met me in the foyer and I followed her into the service room, tripping over a bucket on the way in. We were surrounded by an army of brooms, mops and vacuum cleaners.

'We'll have to stop meeting like this,' I said. 'Wouldn't it be better to meet out in the open to prove to your boyfriend's thug mates that we have nothing to hide?'

Somehow I couldn't bring myself to call him by his first name.

'Eddie wouldn't see it like that. Anyhow, you're the one who wanted to meet in person. We could just as easily talk about this on the phone.'

She had me there. I'd used this as an excuse to see her.

'The truth is I have a plan. It's a good and necessary plan but you're not going to like it, so I thought I should discuss it with you in person, so I'd have a better chance of talking you into it."

She folded her arms across her chest, making her breasts jut out even more. 'Hit me with it and watch me resist your charms.'

'How would you like to do a road trip with me? To Gosford.'

'No friggin' way. I'm going to Gosford on my own, even if I have to quit my job.'

'Let me explain why that's not a good idea. Mind if I sit down? Thanks.'

I removed a pile of wet cloths draped over the side of a bucket, turned it upside down and plonked myself on it.

'If you go down there on your own, you're just one woman demanding information that no-one either can or wants to give you. If you have me as your lawyer with you, I can verify that you're who you say you are and that the reasons for your search are authentic. People will be much more inclined to listen and once they're listening, we've got a much better chance of getting information from them. And my ability to talk to officials without swearing at them is a definite plus, wouldn't you agree?'

Frankie pursed her lips but said nothing.

'There's something else. I told Family and Community Services that you have terminal cancer – it was the only way I could persuade them to tell me what town Jake had lived in. And I think I've found the high school he went to, but of course they couldn't reveal that. So if we fronted up in person with that story, we might persuade them to give us some information.'

Frankie stared at me, open-mouthed. 'You told them I'm dying? You, a fine upstanding lawyer, told an outright lie?'

There was more than a hint of ironic amusement in her eyes. I'd been wrestling with that question myself. Not only had I lied, but I'd also breached my code of ethics.

I shrugged. 'Let's hope the end justifies the means. My going to Gosford with you is your best hope, Frankie.'

She looked away. Her hair glinted red under the fluorescent lights of the service room. I imagined it let loose from under her cap, tumbling over her bare neck, soft as feathers. I imagined running my fingers through it and pressed my hands firmly onto my knees.

'What if Eddie finds out?'

'How would he find out? Have someone tail us all the way to Gosford?'

'He'd find out, believe me.'

I thought quickly. 'Okay, here's what we'll do. See if you can get a couple of days off work during the week, say Monday to Wednesday. We have to go while school's on. I'll pick you up in a pre-arranged spot, somewhere in the city where it's crowded. Where do you live?'

'Bankstown.'

'Quite a way to travel to work.'

'Eddie's mum lives in Bondi Junction. I stay with her when I'm working on this side of town. Saves me quite a bit of money in fuel.'

'If you catch a train to Central, I'll meet you near the station. If you really think you're going to be followed, go into the Ladies and change into a disguise. Wear a fat suit or a false nose if you have to.'

Frankie refused to smile. 'Where would we stay?'

'We'll find a motel somewhere.'

'You'll have to book separate rooms.'

'Of course.'

I could see her weighing up the stakes – the desire to find her brother vs. possible repercussions from Eddie if he found out she'd gone away in the company of another man.

She met my gaze. 'This is going to cost you money. And time.'

'Yes.'

'I still don't know why you're doing this.'

'It's a refreshing change for me. I'm quite enjoying being a private investigator.'

It was true. Right now, looking for Jacob was proving much more exciting than financial spreadsheets, filing papers for court and interpreting bankruptcy law. But that wasn't the only reason. Or even the main reason. While my head was telling me this relationship, platonic though it was, would lead me into unknown and probably dangerous territory, the rest of me wanted to hurtle on regardless. I was incapable of stopping.

'And you do this for all your pro bono clients?'

'What can I say? I'm a generous guy.'

'I guess I can't argue with that.' She looked at her watch. 'Gotta go. I'll work on my boss to get some time off. It's going to be tough though; he's one hell of a mean bastard.'

'Use your feminine wiles. I know it's not politically correct, but desperate times call for desperate measures.'

We parted ways at the entrance of the resort. 'Where are you off to now?' I asked her.

'To the pub.' She grinned. 'Seeing as I haven't got long to live, I'm partying hard.'

Chapter 10

'So William, how are things in the bankruptcy world?' Vera Longhurst yelled in my ear above the din of conversation and music in the private function room of the Grand Chancellor Hotel.

'Booming!' I yelled back. 'Lots of people going broke, so there's lots of business.'

She nodded in that vacant way people do when they haven't listened to a word you've said. 'Nick's doing very well, isn't he? Fancy getting the opportunity to work in the International Court in The Hague! Such a step up for his career. And Stephanie getting that scholarship to the United States! That's all your mother could talk about when she picked me up from the airport. I must go and find some more of those darling little pastries.'

She swept off in a cloud of perfume. I downed my beer. I was well used to people, including my parents and Mum's cousin Vera, trumpeting the achievements of my older brother and younger sister over mine. It had hurt for a long time until I decided I was too mature to let it worry me. Most of the time.

Uncle Howard squeezed my shoulder as he passed. 'How are you going, young Will? Your mother's looking fantastic, isn't she?"

I looked over at Mum, holding court to a bevy of well-coiffured, bejewelled women and boozy, hearty men. This was her party, the occasion of her 60th birthday; and even from a son's point of view, she looked pretty good. She worked hard to maintain her slimness and her face didn't have that hard, cynical edge I saw in a lot of her friends. Dad was beside her, ostensibly joining in the conversation; but his hawk-like eyes constantly scanned the room to see if there was anyone of influence he should be talking to.

Someone shoved another beer at me. 'How's it going, bro?'

Steph was beside me, looking glamorous in a cocktail dress with her blonde hair in a French knot.

'Better now I've got another beer, thanks. I suppose Dad's going to give another one of his speeches, addressing us all as if we're members of the jury.'

Steph grinned. 'Guilty as charged. You haven't forgotten dinner at the olds' on Tuesday night?'

'Is it next Tuesday?'

She punched me.

'Of course I'm coming. Wouldn't miss a last chance to have a couple of bourbons with you.'

'And you're coming to the airport on Wednesday morning?'

'You bet. Got to make sure you actually get on the plane.'

I felt my phone vibrate in my pocket. I pulled it out. 'Frankie' was lit up on the screen. Steph peered over my shoulder. 'Who's Frankie? Have you turned gay on us?'

'It's a woman. 'Scuse me, I have to take this.'

'Hang on, Frankie, I'll just get out of the noise,' I said, as I pushed my way through the crowd and out the glass doors onto the terrace.

'Am I interrupting something?' Frankie asked.

'It's my mother's 60th birthday. But I've got time to talk.'

'I've got three days off work, from Wednesday to Friday next week. That's the only time the boss would give me because he's got someone who can cover me for those days.'

Damn. It wasn't a good time – I'd miss seeing Steph off on Wednesday and I had a court appearance on Thursday for a client. But what the hell, I didn't want her to lose her job.

'That's fine. I'll call you tomorrow and we'll organise it.'

#

I told Louis I had to take some urgent holiday leave for family reasons. His brow rumpled.

'Is everything all right?'

'My sister's leaving next week for a couple of years in the States and my mother's not taking it very well.' It was too lame, even though it was the truth, so I added, 'and to make matters worse, my father's just had a heart attack.'

It could easily happen, I told myself, to ease the niggle of guilt in my gut. He was a sitting duck – overweight, no exercise and a workaholic. Even in his down time as Head of Law at the University of Sydney, he was doing research and writing academic papers.

It was obvious Louis was irritated about the disruption this would cause but trying not to show it in the name of compassion. 'All right, brief Jared on what you've got happening next week. It will be a good opportunity to see what he's made of.'

Jared was our graduate law student, who'd only been with the company a few months. I briefed him on my main project, an upcoming court case involving a large construction firm, which had been declared bankrupt. The firm was owned by two brothers of Italian descent; each was accusing the other of financial mismanagement. I'd secretly nicknamed them The Bankruptcy Brothers; and at a recent meeting with them in my office, I'd had to step in to avert a brawl. I always seemed to end up with the cases that involved family disputes.

'My advice is don't let them get a word in edgeways,' I told Jared. 'Compared to their antics, court will be a no-brainer.'

As I was due to do my gig on Friday night at The Three Monkeys, I phoned Sarah and cancelled for that night just in case we weren't back in time. There were plenty of performers who could fill in for me.

'Where are you off to?' Sarah asked.

'Er – just to the Central Coast. With a friend.'

Which was true. Although Frankie probably wouldn't call me a friend.

'It's about time you had a holiday. I'll see you in a couple of weeks, all relaxed and with a tan.'

Somehow I doubted that.

#

I steeled myself for the inquisition at the family dinner. We were seated around the dining room table – my parents, Nick and his wife Jaclyn, Steph and me – and were just about to tuck into our Atlantic salmon and asparagus salad when my father fixed me with his formidable gaze.

'And you couldn't put your holiday off for just a couple of hours to see your sister off at the airport?'

I could have, but Frankie and I wanted to get an early start in the morning – we had to make maximum use of the time we had. Anyway, I hate airport goodbyes – all the waiting around, everyone trying to better each other at travel disaster stories, and trying not to cry. But whatever I said would be inadequate.

'You're going away with Frankie, aren't you?' Steph asked.

My mother raised a well-manicured brow. 'Who's Frankie?

'Just a friend I'm helping out.'

Nick smirked. 'That's a new name for it. Back in my day we called it a dirty weekend.'

'Bonus points if it's during the week,' he added.

Jaclyn giggled dutifully as she picked at her meal. She was four months pregnant with their first child, not that you could tell, and she was determined not to put on an ounce more than necessary.

I gave Nick my 'you're-so-lame' look, which he ignored as usual. At thirty-four, his belly was already thickening and with the same shaggy hair and features as Dad, it was easy to see exactly what he would be like in thirty years' time.

'What did you think of the Anderson case in London?' Dad asked Nick, changing the conversation to something more stimulating than my supposed love life.

After dessert, I went into the kitchen to help Mum make the coffee.

'I'm glad you've got a girlfriend, dear,' she said, as she poured boiling water into the plunger. 'I was very concerned about you after Angelique left you. You took it very hard. I hope you don't mind me saying so, but I never did like her. She was very charming, but there was something not quite genuine about her. I thought you could do better.'

My relationships report card – Will tries hard with women but could do better.

'You'll have to bring Frankie over for dinner one night.'

I suppressed a smile. Frankie with her skinny jeans, heavy make-up and every second word being 'fuck'. And ducking outside every half hour for a cigarette. It would be almost worth it to see the expression on my father's face.

'She's just a friend, Mum, there's nothing between us.'

She gave me one of her 'you-can't-fool-me, I'm-your-mother' smiles and handed me a tray of coffee mugs.

\#

As I pulled up in my garage, I heard my phone signal a text message. I waited until I was inside before opening it. Unknown number. 'Stay away from Eddie's missus pretty boy or I'll come after you and you won't look so pretty.'

I was tired and had intended to go straight to bed. Instead I made myself another coffee and sat on the front deck. It wasn't just the sea breeze that chilled me to my core. How did this anonymous piece of shit know of my contact with Frankie? Perhaps she was right after all and Eddie had organised for one of his so-called mates to follow her, which had led them to me. Was there someone following me as well? Or tapping my phone? All my contact with Frankie had been on my mobile phone. I knew it was possible to tap a mobile phone, but it required a level of technical expertise that I doubted a run-of-the-mill thug would have access to.

I was wide awake when I eventually went to bed, all those questions still churning in my mind. I couldn't cancel the trip to Gosford now – Frankie was relying on me to help her and I couldn't let her down. I wouldn't have time to report the message to the police before we left in the morning, although how much they could find out was questionable. If the sender had even a modicum of sense, the phone they used to send the message would have been purchased under a false name and discarded as soon as it was used.

The other possibility was that the message was a bluff, on the assumption it would be enough to scare me off without having to 'come after me'. But even if it wasn't a bluff and someone did follow us, what could they do? Shoot us in broad daylight?

I resolved to be extra vigilant for both Frankie and myself, and make sure we didn't leave ourselves vulnerable to attack.

Chapter 11

At 7 AM, I pulled up in a loading bay a couple of blocks away from Central Station and texted Frankie to tell her where I was. Already the sun was breaking through the cloud and was hovering on the brink of a shiny spring day. I hoped it would lift my mood – I was wrung out after my disturbed night's sleep and early morning. I gulped down the coffee I'd bought on the way from the drive-through at McDonald's. The passenger door was wrenched open and a figure in jeans, bright patchwork coat and boots jumped in. She hauled in her overnight bag and threw it onto the back seat.

'The bloody train was late,' Frankie said. 'And then this guy came and sat next to me, reeking of booze. Just what you need at 6 am.'

She wriggled out of her coat and clicked on her seatbelt. 'Swanky car. Don't think I've ever ridden in an Audi.'

'The boozy guy. Did he get off at Central too?'

'Nope, he went to sleep. Why?'

'Just hoping he didn't hassle you.'

'Bullshit, you thought he might be following me, didn't you? Now who's getting antsy?'

'It must be catching,' I said, trying to keep a casual tone. I'd decided not to tell her about the text message – I didn't want to make her any more frightened than she already was. And she might cease all contact with me, something I definitely didn't want.

'You don't have to worry about that,' she said. 'I got off at Canterbury and walked towards the exit then just as the train was about to take off again, I made a run for it and jumped back on. The door almost closed on top of me; so if anyone was following me, they wouldn't have had time to get back on.'

'Good work,' I said. 'Your talents are wasted - you should be in the MI5.'

'Yeah. In another life it could have been fun.'

As I pulled out into the traffic, she turned around and threw her coat onto the back seat, next to her overnight bag and my guitar in its case.

'You play the guitar?' she asked.

'I thought we could have a singalong after dinner, just to relieve the boredom.'

She looked at me as if not quite sure if I was serious. 'I'll just watch telly, thanks.'

She slumped down in her seat and stared out the window. 'What's that music you're playing?'

'Amy Winehouse. You don't like it?'

'It's too sad. I hate sad music.'

I fast-forwarded on my iPod to Red Hot Chili Peppers, figuring that would be more her taste. When we reached the Pacific Motorway, I put my foot down and we flew past a kaleidoscope of green fields, farmhouses and sheep, as pretty as an illustration in a child's picture book.

'So, how did you persuade your tyrant of a boss to give you three days off?' I asked.

'I said I had to have a minor operation.'

'He was okay with that?

'I gave him a medical certificate. We need one if we have more than one day off.'

'How did you persuade your doctor to give you that?'

'I didn't, it was forged.'

'Shit, Frankie what did you do that for? What happens if you get caught?'

'Chill out! I had to. It was the only way I could get time off. And I didn't write it, a friend did. Well, not really a friend, just someone I know.'

'That makes no difference ¬– you're still guilty of fraud.'

'I know that! But I won't get caught; he barely even looked at it. And anyway, the end justifies the means.'

Her lips twitched with a self-satisfied smile. I refrained from replying. The strains of The Cure's 'Friday I'm In Love' rang out, and Frankie dug into her handbag and pulled out her phone.

'Hi babe.'

After a couple of minutes she said, 'Yeah, fine.' She glanced at me. 'Just about to leave for work. How are you, anyway?'

A pause. 'I gotta work this weekend, so I can't come out. But next weekend I will, I promise.'

Another silence. 'I'm fine, honest, babe. Don't worry about me.' She gave a stilted laugh. 'Of course I'm not going out – I'm so tired when I get home from work I'm falling asleep in my dinner.'

Then softly, 'Love you too. Talk to you soon.'

She put her phone back in her bag.

'How often does he phone you?' I asked.

'When he's allowed to. Depends which screws are on duty.'

'So how did you two meet?'

'On the dodgem cars at the Royal Easter Show. He kept ramming my car and pretending it was an accident but it was so obvious it wasn't. When we'd finished the ride, I walked away and he came running after me with some fairy floss. So it just kind of went from there.'

'The old sweeten-her-up-with-fairy-floss trick. How long have you been together?'

I remembered too late that in court David Levenson had said they'd been together for seven years.

'I was eighteen when we met, so seven years – on and off.'

'Anyway,' she added belligerently, 'what business is it of yours?'

'None whatsoever. I promise I won't ask any more questions.''

Frankie rummaged in her handbag, took out an iPod, stuck the earplugs in her ear and stared out the window again. I got the message and didn't initiate any further conversation. In any case, I was preoccupied with checking the rear view mirror to see if we were being followed. If we were, they were too far back for me to notice.

#

We arrived at Gosford at 8.30 am. We were both ready for breakfast by then, so I stopped at a bakery and bought us both a coffee and croissant. There was a chemist next door, and on impulse I went in and bought a packet of face wipes. When I got back into the car, I handed them to Frankie.

'You'll have to take your make-up off. You look far too healthy.'

'But I look crap without make-up!'

'You're supposed to look crap – you're terminally ill, remember?'

She sighed heavily and tore open the packet, took out a wipe and rubbed it over her face. She surveyed herself in the passenger mirror. 'I've left a bit of eye make-up on. It looks better – more of a contrast.'

She turned her face to me. She was right. The eyeliner she'd left on emphasised her pale, wan complexion. Her lips looked colourless without their usual iridescent lipstick, but they were full and perfectly shaped. Without her make-up, she looked defenceless – I felt as if I were seeing the real Frankie, that I could look inside her and see her soul. I sensed she felt it too as she turned her head away, slid her croissant out of the paper bag and began munching.

I demolished my breakfast as I drove along the busy streets, which every now and then flashed a teasing glimpse of the shimmering turquoise ocean. The dulcet directions of my GPS led us to the Northwoods State Secondary College. It was bedlam – cars and buses banked up and packs of students swarming everywhere. I found a car park a couple of blocks down the road and turned off the engine.

'This is the plan,' I said. 'We're going up to the administration centre and hopefully Amanda, the woman I talked to on the phone, will be there. And let's hope the principal won't be hovering around. I'll do all the talking, and your job is to say nothing and look as if you're on death's doorstep.'

'I could have got a medical certificate for me having cancer,' Frankie said.

'The same way you got the other one? No way. I've already lied and misrepresented myself, and I don't fancy breaking the law as well.'

'Fine, Mr Upright Citizen, let's see how far your charms get you.'

I gulped down the rest of my coffee and brushed the croissant crumbs off me. 'Okay, let's do it.'

At the school entrance, we followed the signs to the administration block. Classes had obviously started as most of the students had disappeared, except for a few stragglers. A fiercely efficient-looking woman at the front counter gave us the once-over.

'Can I help you?'

I knew she wasn't Amanda even before I spotted her name tag – Myra.

'Good morning, Myra. I'm Will McPherson, I'm a solicitor and this is my client Francis Slater. Is Amanda available?'

'Amanda's not in today,' she said curtly. 'What's it concerning?'

Plan B needed. What was plan B?

'It's a rather delicate matter,' I said. 'Is there someone we can talk to in private?'

She studied Frankie, no doubt trying to work out whose parent she was. 'Is it about your child, Ms Slater?'

Frankie shook her head.

'Ms Slater doesn't have a child at this school,' I said.

She raised her eyebrows. 'I'm sorry, that's all I can say,' I said.

A brief look of concern flitted across her face. I'd made it sound rather sinister – she was probably thinking it was not good news if there was a lawyer involved.

'The principal's in a meeting but the deputy could probably see you. Is that all right?'

'That's fine.'

She disappeared and came back accompanied by a short, red-haired woman in a tailored suit. 'Good morning, I'm Lyn Andrews, the deputy principal.'

I introduced us both and we all shook hands. Her handshake was firm and businesslike. We followed her into her office, a small room dwarfed by an expansive desk.

She took her seat behind it and motioned for us to sit down. What she lacked in height she made up for in presence. She wasn't going to be a pushover.

'So, you're a solicitor, Mr McPherson. Are you going to sue us?'

Right to the point. I decided to take a leaf out of her book. 'No, I'm not going to sue you, but I am going to ask you to consider a request which is a little unusual and against your code of ethics. But I consider the end justifies the means.'

Frankie shifted in her chair and I sensed her inner smirk.

'No doubt Hitler had the same point of view,' Lyn said, 'but I'm intrigued, so tell me what it is so at least I know what I'm refusing.'

I told her Frankie's story, from the time Jake was taken away from the family through to her failed attempts to find him. I recounted the facts, leaving out the emotion.

'And now, Ms Slater has just been given the diagnosis of stomach cancer – she's about to start chemotherapy but it's just delaying the inevitable. The doctors have given her 12 months. I met her through another client and she asked me to help her track down her brother as she desperately wants to find him before she passes away. I managed to find out that he was adopted by a foster family living in Gosford and I have an inkling he went to this school. His name was Jacob Van Graf but he was adopted when he was 12, so his name may have been changed to that of his foster family. I know you're not permitted to release information about students, but this school is our only lead. If we can find out what address he was living at while he was here, that gives us somewhere to start from.'

From my briefcase I took out the Adoption Information Certificate that Frankie had given me and handed it to Lyn.

'This is proof that Ms Slater is his sister and that she's authorised to seek information about him.'

She glanced at it. 'You do realise what you're asking me to do, Mr McPherson? You're not only asking me to breach the school's confidentiality but the foster family's confidentiality as well.'

'I'm fully aware of that, and of course I wouldn't divulge my sources – not even under torture.'

Lyn didn't smile. She was looking at Frankie.

'Ms Slater, have you ever considered that if you find your brother he might not want to know you? You might think that couldn't happen, but you don't know him now – children change as they grow up, sometimes dramatically.'

Frankie shrugged. 'I'd do the bossy big sister thing and try my hardest to persuade him, but if he really didn't want to see me...' her voice trailed away and she swallowed hard, 'at least I'd have given it my best shot.'

'So it would give you closure?'

'Closure! That's such a bullshit word!' Frankie spat out. 'Nothing will ever give me closure, not even finding him.

Nothing will change the fact that he was taken away from me and nothing can bring back those years we missed.'

For God's sake shut up. Frankie glanced at me then said, 'Sorry for swearing, but I meant every word.'

She took her wallet out of her handbag, slipped out the crumpled photo of her and Jake as children and placed it on the desk in front of Lyn. Lyn's expression remained unchanged as she studied the photo then passed it wordlessly back to Frankie. This wasn't going to plan. Lyn didn't strike me as the sort of person whose heartstrings would be moved by baby photos, or by being sworn at, for that matter.

The phone on her desk rang. 'Hullo ... all right, I'll just look it up and be right there.'

She tapped away on her computer for a few seconds then got up. 'Excuse me, there's something I have to attend to. I'll be back shortly.'

She closed the door behind her. Frankie and I looked at each other.

'Did I blow it?' Frankie asked.

Probably.

'Probably not,' I said. 'She's a hard nut to crack.'

Frankie stood up, leaned over the desk and looked at the computer monitor.

'Sit down for God's sake, before she comes back.'

'No, Will, look!' She turned the monitor around to face us. We were looking at a spreadsheet entitled 'Year 12 Students 2000.' It was in alphabetical order and just over halfway down the page was the name Jacob Magarry. Date of birth 06/06/1983. Address 20 Glenfields Road, North Gosford. And a phone number as well.

'It's Jake!' she said. 'Different surname but same date of birth.'

I grabbed a notebook and pen from my briefcase, and scribbled down the address and phone number. Frankie was still studying the information. 'He was in 12A and scored 95 for his final results. That's pretty damn good! I never even started year 12. And look, he did physics and chemistry. My brother is a genius!'

Her face shone with pride. I put my hand gently on her arm. 'We have to pretend we didn't see this; that's why she's done it this way.'

I turned the screen around and we sat back in our seats. 'Don't forget to look sick,' I whispered, as the door opened and Lyn bustled back in.

'Sorry for the interruption.' She remained standing. 'I'm sure you both appreciate that despite your unfortunate circumstances, Ms Slater, I can't give you the information you've requested. But I wish you well.'

She faltered for a moment as she realised what she'd said, then stood aside to let us out. We shook hands again.

'Thank you for your time anyway, Ms Andrews.'

I winked at her to let her know we'd got what we wanted.

We were silent till we got out the front gate. Then Frankie shrieked and wrapped her arms around me. 'That was fucking great! I take it back about your charms!'

I laughed. 'I think somehow it might have been your dubious charms that did it.'

Her body was deliciously warm and soft against mine and it wasn't just her perfume that was making my head spin.

She pulled herself away from me abruptly. 'Let's go there now.'

Chapter 12

Frankie rang the phone number I'd written down; but as expected, it had been disconnected. I punched the address into the GPS – it was only a few streets away. As we drove, Frankie was silent. I guessed she was mulling over the new information about Jake.

'His adopted family must have been good for him,' she said. 'You don't usually get good results at school if you're unhappy. He did better than me, the lucky bastard.'

'You weren't happy with your foster family?'

'Families, I lost count of how many I had. A couple were okay.'

Chasms unspoken, but now was not the time to probe. Number 20 was a low-set, shabby brick home. A pushbike and two skateboards were flung across the front lawn. It had an air of lifelessness about it, and there was no answer to the doorbell.

'There's obviously someone living here,' I said. 'Let's come back at six o'clock and hopefully we'll catch them home.'

Frankie walked around the side of the house and peered in through a window.

'Come on, stickybeak.'

'I want to see what his house is like.'

'His family might have moved from here,' I pointed out.

'I know, but even if they have, he lived here once. I know it sounds stupid, but I want to feel his presence.'

I waited in the car for her as she stood at the fence staring at the home, hoping the neighbours wouldn't think we were casing the joint. When she got in I said, 'It's too early to check into the motel. What do you want to do?'

'Let's go to the beach,' Frankie said. 'I want to feel the sand under my feet.'

It occurred to me it would be safer if we hung out where there were crowds, for example, a shopping centre. It would be harder to ascertain if anyone was following us but also harder for someone to rearrange my 'pretty face'. I'd continued to check my rear vision since arriving in Gosford but hadn't spied any suspicious vehicles. And the beach sounded much more inviting.

As I headed towards the ocean, Frankie checked Facebook on her phone for Jake Magarry. There were only two – one was the wrong age, the other was born in the United States. She also looked up the White Pages phone book, but there were no Magarrys in Gosford.

'They could have an unlisted number,' I pointed out. 'Or not even have a landline at all.'

'Yeah, I guess so. I suppose I should be thankful he has a fairly unusual surname – imagine if it was Brown or Smith!'

I parked in front of a small beach nestled into a rocky headland, sprinkled with sun worshippers spreadeagled on the sand, invoking the sun god to transform their pasty winter skin into a golden summer tan.

The day was clear and light, and full of hope. We took off our shoes and I walked sedately along, relishing the solidity of the wet sand under my bare feet. It had been a long time since I'd walked barefoot on the sand, despite living a stone's throw from the ocean. Frankie rolled up her jeans and paddled in the shallows. When we reached the rock wall, she turned to me.

'Let's go in.'

Without waiting for my reply, she threw off her shirt, yanked her jeans down and stood before me in her underwear. 'You coming?' Her mouth curved provocatively. 'You *are* wearing underpants?'

She turned and raced into the water, hair streaming behind her. I was surprised at how well filled out her body was for someone so thin – the muscular thinness of an athlete. She dived into a wave and came up spluttering and laughing.

'Come on in, it's magic!' She jumped a wave and her breasts bounced in their black lacy confines then she caught another and bodysurfed into shore. What sort of woman goes swimming in black lacy underwear? Someone who's trying to bait me?

But Frankie's exuberance was childlike and she was either oblivious or uncaring about her effect on anyone else. I had a feeling she would have done the same, regardless of whose company she was in. I wanted to join her, to prove I wasn't the stick-in-the-mud I suspected she thought I was, but watching her frolicking half naked had caused me to be in a state of arousal, which would be rather obvious once I removed my jeans. I sat down on the sand and tried to think unsexy thoughts. Tax, bankruptcy, the enormous hairy wart on my Aunt Edith's chin. Anything except my fantasy of a rogue breaker ripping off Frankie's underwear.

Frankie's head bobbed up from the water and she waved to me. 'Come on, party pooper! You can't come to the beach and not go for a swim!'

'I'm working up to it!' I called back. She turned round and dived under a wave. Now was my chance. I pulled off my shirt, unzipped my jeans, stepped out of them and raced into the water before she had time to surface again. The coldness hit me with such intensity it took my breath away. 'Holy Jesus, it's freezing!'

Frankie turned around and grinned. 'Wimp!'

My body was now completely numb and my balls had shrivelled to the size of prunes. Any sexy thoughts had been put into a cryogenic state, to be resurrected later. After a few minutes of bodysurfing, I was warm enough to start enjoying myself. At Frankie's suggestion we had a series of swimming races, which she won hands down, gliding effortlessly through the water like a dolphin.

'Swimming was never my strong point,' I said. 'I'm more of a land animal.'

In that strange way in which time seems to expand when you're in the water, it seemed as if we were there for at least an hour, but it was probably only half that time. We sat on the sand in the sun drying ourselves off. The sea breeze tickled my wet skin and gave me goosebumps. I glanced at Frankie and noticed she had goosebumps as well – all over her, including her nipples. I hastily averted my eyes. *Don't you dare!* I silently warned my penis.

'I know one way to get warm,' she said, jumping up. 'Let's have a race. To the rock wall and back. From that pile of seaweed.' She pointed to it, about 100 metres down the beach.

I didn't fancy running up and down the beach in my underpants. Particularly as I'd just realised I was wearing one of my older pairs, which sported a couple of holes.

She gave me a taunting look. 'Come on, land animal.'

I gave a mock groan. 'If I race you, will you leave me alone so I can build a sand castle?'

'Sure thing.'

At the pile of seaweed, I drew a line in the sand with my foot.

'Wait a minute,' Frankie said.

'Excuse me!' she called out to a man who was approaching us. He was short and wiry with dreadlocks, wearing only a pair of board shorts. His skin was leathery brown underneath an elaborate artwork of tattoos. He was throwing a stick to his portly golden labrador, who bounded after it with the grace of a pregnant elephant.

'We're having a race,' Frankie said. 'Can you be the referee?'

Dreadlocks looked us both up and down, his glance flickering over my holey underpants then coming to rest on Frankie. He looked like one of the old-school surfies from way back when it was cool to surf all day and smoke bongs all night.

'Whaddya need a referee for?' he drawled. 'Are you training for the Olympics?'

'We need an objective third party.' Frankie jerked her thumb in my direction. 'He's a lawyer; he's bound to find a loophole somewhere.'

'You're obviously scared I'm going to beat you,' I said.

'Not at all,' Frankie said. 'Just want to avoid any disputes. Isn't that what lawyers are supposed to do?'

'All right, children, enough arguing!' Dreadlocks was getting into the spirit of it. 'Line up and when I say 'bang!' you go.'

We lined up. Dreadlocks pointed an imaginary starter pistol in the air. 'Ready, steady, BANG!'

Frankie took off like a greyhound with a firecracker under her. I soon caught up and so did the labrador, racing beside us, excited to be in on this new game. On the home run Frankie was just a smidge in front of me and the dog. I put on a final burst of energy – my pride was at stake here. I was not going to be beaten by a woman and /or an overweight labrador.

It seemed to me that Frankie and I reached the line at exactly the same second, with the labrador a close second. But the referee disagreed.

'First prize to the Lady in Black!' he called, giving her an appraising once-over.

'Come on!' I said. 'That was a tie!'

'See?' Frankie said triumphantly, 'I told you he'd object!'

'It was definitely the lady,' Dreadlocks said. 'Her tits were over the line first.'

'Sorry,' he added to Frankie. 'Hope I didn't offend you.'

Frankie grinned. 'Not at all.'

'Unfair advantage, ' I protested.

'Referee's decision is final,' Dreadlocks said. 'You two lovebirds will have to fight it out in the bedroom.'

'We're not lovebirds,' Frankie said. 'He's my lawyer.'

'Whatever,' Dreadlocks said, giving me a knowing look. I had to admit, the evidence for that statement wasn't convincing. How many people had races on the beach in their underwear with their lawyer?

Being well and truly dry now, we put our clothes back on.

'If we were in a court of law, I'd dispute that decision,' I said. 'I think the referee was blinded by your obvious assets. But as we're not, I'm willing to gracefully concede defeat.'

'Big of you,' Frankie said, buttoning her shirt over her assets.

'And to prove it, I'll shout you lunch.'

As we walked up the beach towards the café across the road, I said, 'You're a natural athlete.'

'It was the only thing I was good at at school. I was a bit of a tomboy as a kid. I was the only girl the boys would allow on their soccer team. I could run faster than most of them and if they teased me about being a girl, I'd knock them out.'

I grinned. 'Why doesn't that surprise me?'

We bought fish and chips and went back to the beach to eat them, finding a secluded spot near the rock wall. It occurred to me that if Gisbourne had his spies watching us, it would be easy for them to get the wrong idea.

My appetite had been sharpened by the exercise and sea air, and I couldn't remember the last time I'd tasted anything as delicious as the fresh, tender fish and the chips cooked to crispy perfection. Frankie ate voraciously, licking the salt off her fingers.

A flock of expectant seagulls gathered around us. She threw a chip to one of them and laughed as they all squabbled over it.

'That's the first time I've heard you laugh,' I said.

'Maybe I don't have a lot to laugh about.'

'I can understand that. How do you cope, with your boyfriend in jail?'

'What you really mean is, how do I cope without sex.'

'I guess that's part of it. But it wasn't what I was specifically asking.'

'Don't bullshit me. If you were a woman, maybe not, but when guys ask me that question, what they really want to know is what I do when I'm horny.'

'And what do you tell them?'

'I tell them to mind their own fucking business because they're usually thinking that I must be so desperate for a shag that I'll take anyone who asks, which means them.'

'You need to hang out with a better class of man,' I said.

'Like you, for example?'

'Why not? Women have been known to phone me and wait for days for the chance to see me in person. By the time I've gone through all the clauses of section 56B of the Bankruptcy Act, they're practically ripping my clothes off.'

She burst out laughing and I laughed at her laughter. It was one of those moments of connection when you feel at one with every living thing, and all is right with the universe.

#

At the Sandy Beach Motel we were booked into rooms 10 and 11. It overlooked the ocean but our rooms were at the back, with no view. Frankie disappeared into her room to have an afternoon nap and I made a cup of instant sawdust from the supplied coffee sachets and watched an old James Bond movie on TV. I peered out the window several times, checking the car park and surrounds for vehicles that looked familiar or suspicious, though I really didn't have a clue what I was looking for and felt like a paranoid, curtain-twitching old biddy.

Frankie knocked on my door at a quarter to six. She'd changed into a summery dress and a lacy cardigan. Her hair was out in all its glorious mess and she looked as if she'd just stepped out of a Scandinavian ad for shampoo.

'Wow! What a transformation!' I said.

She looked sheepish. 'I just thought ... in case he's there...'

In the car on the way to the house, I said, 'I'll wait in the car, if you want.'

She didn't reply but as we pulled up in front, she said,'
I'd like you to come with me, if you don't mind.'

I felt warm all over inside, though I was nervous for her
as well. Daylight saving had begun and the afternoon was
still clear and bright. A battered, early model Toyota was
parked in the carport. As we stood at the front door, the
insistent blaring of a TV mingled with children's screams.
Frankie took a deep breath and pressed the doorbell. After a
few moments, the door was whipped open by a lumpy,
harassed-looking woman. The noise from inside was
deafening.

'Hi,' Frankie said. 'Sorry to bother you. Does Jake
Magarry still live here?'

'The Magarrys moved about four years ago.'

She turned around and yelled, 'Will youse kids stop that
racket!'

'Do you know where they went?' Frankie said.

'They went to Avalon, but I dunno if they're still there.'

'Did they leave a forwarding address?' I asked.

She narrowed her eyes. 'Are youse the cops?'

'No,' I said, 'we're friends of Jake's, we want to catch up
with him.'

She looked at us disbelievingly. 'Nope, got no idea.'

And slammed the door in our faces.

Chapter 13

Frankie and I looked at each other.

'First time I've ever been asked if I'm a cop,' Frankie said.

'Me too.'

As we got back in the car, Frankie said, 'Where's Avalon?'

'It's a little coastal town – I don't think it's far from here.'

Frankie looked it up on her phone as I drove off. 'It's 82 kilometres to Avalon Beach. I'll see if I can find any Magarrys in the White Pages.'

After a minute she said, 'Hey, what do you know? There's a C and L Magarry in Avalon. 26 Seagull Ave. The only Magarrys there – that has to be them.'

'It looks promising,' I agreed. 'It will probably take us an hour and a bit to get to Avalon, so it's a bit late in the day to turn up out of the blue on their doorstep. What about giving them a call?'

Frankie shook her head. 'I don't think we should ring them at all. It's too easy for people to tell you to piss off on the phone. I think we should just turn up on the doorstep first thing tomorrow morning.'

I wasn't so sure it was a good idea to turn up without warning – it could put the Magarrys offside. But I said nothing. From now on, it was Frankie's call.

As we pulled into the motel car park I said, 'Do you want to go somewhere for dinner?'

'Is this on the pro bono expense account as well?'

'Of course. Rest assured all these expenses are tax deductible.' Even if they weren't, I didn't care.

The motel restaurant was cramped and noisy, so we walked a couple of blocks to the Empire Hotel bar and grill, an unpretentious but cosy restaurant that served the usual pub fare.

As I ordered our meals at the counter and bought our drinks from the bar, I surveyed the other clientele for anyone who looked as if they didn't quite fit in and might be staking us out. But as there were a number of people who could have fitted that description, I gave up. If there was anyone following us, they were too damn efficient at their job.

I handed Frankie her wine and clinked my beer to her glass. 'Here's to finding Jake.'

'To finding Jake,' she echoed.

'I don't want to put a damper on things, but have you considered what Lyn Andrews said? That Jake might not want to see you? Or even that his adopted family might not know where he is, or that he might be living in another country?'

Frankie nodded. 'I have thought about it, but I don't want to dwell on it because it might not happen. I'd rather wait and see, and then if I can't see him for some reason, I'll deal with it then.'

It sounded a reasonable way to look at the situation if I didn't suspect that Frankie was simply avoiding the issue, and that she still expected that she and Jake would run into each other's arms, as if the years dividing them had disappeared on sight.

'So tell me about Jake,' I said. 'What do you remember about him?'

'Everything,' Frankie said. 'Sometimes at night when I'm having trouble sleeping I'll imagine myself back to my childhood. I'm six and Jake is four and we're sitting on the back porch waiting for Mum to get drunk and pass out so we can play Tarzan. There was a vine hanging over the porch and we'd hold on to it and jump off the railing. I'd always insist on being Tarzan and Jake had to be Jane. He hated it but he always gave in.'

I smiled. 'I can just see you bossing him round mercilessly.'

'Don't worry, he got his own back. I had a phobia about grasshoppers – still do, horrible gangly things. My mistake was letting Jake find out. He'd collect them then put one down my back when my guard was down. They were the only times I ever got really mad at him.'

'Sounds like a typical sibling relationship. My younger sister annoyed the hell out of me when we were kids but we're pretty close now.'

Frankie traced a finger down the condensation on her glass. 'It was more than just a brother-sister relationship. I was his mother as well. Jake had just turned two when Tom left Mum and she sank into this really depressive state, drinking all day and hardly even seemed to notice us – only to yell at us for doing something wrong. Most of the time it was me who looked after Jake, dressed him, fed him and kept him amused. When I started school I'd pretend to be sick a lot so Mum would let me stay home, because I knew if I didn't, Jake wouldn't be looked after properly. In the end, that was why the child safety officers came out, because I'd missed so much school.'

'It doesn't sound like much of a childhood.'

'I didn't know any different at the time. When you're a kid you just think your family's nothing out of the ordinary. It's only later when you get to see what other families are like that you realise how fucked up yours was.'

She looked around. 'When's this steak coming?'

Right on cue, our meals arrived – we'd both ordered the rump steak and garlic mash. Frankie demolished every morsel of food on her plate, even the sprig of parsley, and finished my garlic mash as well. She then picked up the menu to peruse the desserts.

'I've never known a woman to eat so much,' I said. 'Where do you put it all?'

She shrugged. 'I burn it all up – nervous energy. Mum used to tell me I had a tapeworm in my stomach and I believed her. That was my excuse when she caught me with my hand in the biscuit jar – I was feeding the tapeworm.'

'Did you have any contact with her after you went into the foster home?'

Frankie shook her head. 'She was too far gone into the alcohol – I don't think she was capable of thinking of anything except where her next drink was coming from. She died of cirrhosis of the liver when I was 15. A woman from the Department came out to my foster home to break the news to me. I'd been so angry with her for so many years for abandoning us, then when I heard she was dead, I just felt numb. The picture I had of her in my mind had faded over the years and I got to the point where I couldn't see her face at all. And I thought, how can I hate her when I can't even remember what she looks like?'

Her voice wavered. She put the menu down and stood up. 'I'm going outside to have a cigarette.'

I finished my drink and ordered another for both of us, by which time Frankie had returned. She reeked of cigarette smoke, which I tried to ignore. In any case, it seemed to have worked as her face had softened and her eyes were brighter.

After dessert and another wine, Frankie was even laughing at my stock of what Steph calls my 'Dad jokes'. When she laughed, her face looked fuller, as if she'd just had a collagen injection, and her eyes lost their defensive expression. The change mesmerised me and I tried hard not to stare.

'You're really different,' Frankie said. 'I've never met a lawyer with a sense of humour. Not that I've met that many,' she added. 'Only Legal Aid lawyers.'

'Some of us hide it well,' I said. 'But a sense of humour is imperative. Do you know any other profession that has a whole category of jokes, all told at its expense? It's why when lawyers die, they're always buried under 20 feet of dirt."

Frankie looked puzzled.

'Because deep down they're really good people.'

Frankie groaned. 'I take that back about your sense of humour.' She cocked her head on one side. 'Do you like being a lawyer?'

Her question took me aback. No-one else had ever asked it. People assumed you liked being a lawyer; otherwise you wouldn't be one. Or you liked the money, which in the eyes of most amounted to the same thing.

The disquiet in my subconscious that I'd suppressed for so long came to the fore. The answer was there in all its simple, perfect clarity. 'No,' I said.

'I thought so.'

'How did you work that out?'

She shrugged. 'Women's intuition. When you talk about your work, it's like you're detached from it, as if it's something you have to do, rather than want to do.'

I considered her remark. Was that how I came across to my clients as well?

'What about you?' I asked to change the subject. 'Do you like cleaning?'

'I don't dislike it – it's a way of earning money. Better than a lot of jobs and you get to work on your own a lot, which I like."

'You seem pretty intelligent – have you ever thought about doing more study?'

'Like what?'

'I don't know. What are your interests?' I thought of the classic question the vocational guidance counsellors ask. 'What did you like doing as a kid?'

She traced her finger around the rim of her wine glass. 'I liked running away to my special hiding place under the house with my favourite book, where my foster father couldn't find me. Could I make a career out of that?'

#

When we got back to the motel, I said, 'I was serious about the singalong. Do you want to come in for a while?'

Frankie hesitated. The walk home had sobered her up a bit and her wariness had returned. 'Okay, but I'm not singing. I'll just listen to you.'

'As long as you don't throw rotten tomatoes.'

Frankie sat on the edge of the second bed while I made us a cup of sawdust each, served up with a cardboard biscuit from a cellophane packet. I took my guitar out of its case and tuned it.

'Here's a little ditty I wrote myself and it goes something like this.'

I played her two of the songs from my album in the making, *Life's a Stage*.

They were both catchy tunes with a good beat and Frankie was soon tapping her foot.

'They're not bad,' she said. 'A bit too folksy for my taste, but you could ramp them up a bit. Play the first one again, a bit faster.'

The first song, 'The Day I Sacked My Best Friend,' was about a young boy who'd discovered his best friend had betrayed him. I sped it up and added more strum to give it a more full-bodied effect. Frankie joined in the chorus. Her voice was mellow with an edge, like a throaty version of Stevie Nicks. And she harmonised perfectly. Her voice gave an extra dimension to the song that I could never have imagined.

As I faded out, Frankie said, 'I'm a bit rusty.'

'You were fantastic. Have you done this professionally? Because if you haven't, you should be.'

'I used to be in a rock band with Eddie – he was the lead guitarist. We called ourselves 'The Heebie Jeebies.' We did the pub scene for a while, but the drugs and alcohol finished it in the end. We were always stoned or pissed, everyone in the scene was, and when the drummer, who was also Eddie's best friend, jumped off a building after dropping acid, it all just fell apart.'

'Do you miss it?'

'What, the drugs and alcohol?' She grinned. 'I gave all that up after the band folded. I could see where it was leading to and I decided to get out while I still had half a brain. But the singing –yeah. I didn't realise how much until just then.'

Come and sing with me, I wanted to say. *We'll make a great duo. You'd give my songs the depth they could never have with just me.*

I played some more of my own stuff. Frankie only needed to hear each song once and she could pick up the melody. If she didn't remember the words, she hummed, which sounded just as good. Then we got into the covers – Powderfinger, Red Hot Chili Peppers, Pearl Jam. As the strains of Pearl Jam's 'Better Man' died away, I noticed in the dim light of the bedside lamp that Frankie's eyes were watery.

'I gotta go.' She jumped up and looped her handbag over her shoulder.

Although I was used to Frankie's abrupt changes of mood, it still jarred me out of my zone.

'I'll see you tomorrow morning – say, seven? We can have breakfast on the way. '

She nodded. I opened the door for her, letting in a gust of cool air.

'Thanks,' she said. I wasn't sure what she was thanking me for. Was it dinner, the music, the night as a whole, or just opening the door for her? I watched her walk to the next-door unit and let herself into number 11.

Chapter 14

We were on our way to Avalon by 7.15 am, stopping halfway at a roadside cafe for a greasy bacon and egg roll and coffee. Frankie only had a couple of bites of her roll. Avalon was a small, sedate coastal town whose main claim to fame was good surf. Although the waves were sparse and choppy, a bunch of optimistic surfers was lined up past the swell, looking like seals in their black wetsuits as they waited for a decent wave.

Twenty-six Seagull Ave was a five minute drive away and one block back from the beach – a two storey brick home, framed by palm trees with a patch of velvety green lawn in front. A late-model Toyota stood in the driveway.

'Someone's home,' I said. I looked at Frankie. She'd hardly said a word all morning. 'Are you nervous?'

'No, but my stomach is.'

I took her hand. It was icy cold. She didn't pull it away.

'Do you want me to come in with you?'

She nodded. At the front door she stood unmoving for some time, then reached out and pressed the doorbell.

The door opened. A man peered out at us. Large, untidy build, rumpled face, thinning hair.

I stepped back to let Frankie do the talking. She cleared her throat. 'Are you Mr Magarry?'

'Yes,' he said warily. 'Who are you?'

'I'm Frankie Slater. I'm Jake's sister.'

He stared at her. 'His ... sister?'

'Half-sister. We were both taken into foster care at the same time but we never had any contact with each other. I never knew where he was and it's taken me all this time to find him.'

'Jesus.' He looked as if he were about to slam the door in our faces, so I stepped forward. 'I can vouch for Frankie, she's telling the truth. I'm Will McPherson, her lawyer. I've been helping her.'

Magarry turned his head and bellowed, 'Leonie, you'd better come here!'

A tall woman with ash-blonde hair appeared in the hallway. He met her halfway and they spoke in low voices. Magarry stepped back as Leonie appeared in the doorway and looked us over. Her warm eyes belied her no-nonsense demeanour. I sensed instantly she'd be good foster mother material.

'How did you find us?' she demanded.

'We can't tell you the specifics,' I said. 'I know you didn't want your identity revealed and I apologise if we've shocked you by turning up out of the blue like this, but Frankie's been so desperate to find Jake that this was the only way. '

'I hope you're not offended, but can I see some ID? I need to be satisfied that you're who you say you are.'

I took a business card from my wallet and handed it to her. Frankie scrabbled around in her handbag and produced her driver's licence. Leonie looked closely at them both and handed them back to us.

'You'd better come in then.'

She ushered us in to a large, airy living room. The decor exuded the old-fashioned comfort of a traditional family home, before marble and glass, and stainless steel became trendy.

'We'd better introduce ourselves,' Leonie said. 'This is my husband, Colin and I'm Leonie.'

We all shook hands. Frankie and I sat side by side on a leather couch, and Colin and Leonie sat in a recliner each. The walls and mantelpiece were adorned with framed family photos. I followed Frankie's gaze to one of a lanky, blonde-haired boy with an infectious grin. He was in a gown and mortar board, holding up a certificate.

'That's Jake at his primary school graduation,' Leonie said. 'He used to call out for you all the time when he first came to us. "Where's Frankie, I want Frankie!" We asked the department if we could arrange contact, but they kept fobbing us off and in the end we gave up. And eventually Jake stopped asking.'

'He did?' Frankie's voice was hoarse.

'Oh, don't worry, he never forgot you. When he turned 18, I suggested he register with the Reunion Register so that if you were looking for him, you could find him; and he assured me that not only would he do that, but that he'd track you down. But... ' She faltered. 'He got caught up doing other things.'

'What sort of things?' Frankie said.

Leonie looked over at Colin, who was leaning forward, hands between his knees, gazing at the floor. He looked up and cleared his throat. 'Jake passed away six months ago.'

Silence. A clock ticked somewhere. Tears rolled down Leonie's face and she made no attempt to brush them away.

'How?' Frankie's voice was barely a whisper.

'Drug overdose,' Colin said. 'We think it was an accident. He'd been off them for a while, trying to stay clean, and then he went to a mate's birthday party and was found in one of the bedrooms the next morning with the needle still in his arm. No one knew he was there – they thought he'd gone home. If I ever find the bastard who gave him that hit...'

Leonie smiled at Frankie through her tears. 'He was such a beautiful boy; a good-looking kid and a real charmer. Smart, too. He got into engineering at University, but decided to take a gap year. Worst thing he ever did. He got a job on a labouring site; they were all into drugs, smoked cannabis on the way to work. Someone introduced him to heroin and that was it. He never made it to Uni.'

'Why, why, why?' Frankie's fists were clenched. 'I was searching for him, waiting for him, why didn't he find me?'

'He had all the best intentions,' Colin said. 'But the best way I can describe it was that he had demons. There was something eating away inside him. I don't know if it was his Dad leaving or being taken away from his mother and you, or all of them and more. He never believed in himself, always thought he was a failure no matter how well he did.'

He got up, picked up a framed photo from the mantelpiece and gave it to Frankie. 'That was his Year 12 graduation.'

A strapping young man in cap and gown smiled out from the photo. His face glowed with the shining optimism and expectancy of youth, though there was a reserve in his eyes that was absent from the younger photo.

'If he wasn't my brother, I'd say he was hot,' Frankie said.

'The girls loved him,' Colin said. 'He was a – what do they call it – chick magnet. But the nice ones all fell away when he started the drugs, and some of the types he brought back here ... in the end we had to forbid him to bring his friends around because we have two younger daughters as well. So of course he left home, so he could hang out with them.'

'Have you got any more photos of him, when he was younger?' Frankie asked.

Leonie and Colin exchanged glances. 'We've got albums full,' Leonie said. 'Would you like to stay for a while and have a cup of tea?"

'I'd love to,' Frankie said.

I stood up. 'I'll leave you here to catch up,' I said to Frankie. I leaned over and gave her a hug. 'I'm so sorry about Jake. Give me a call when you're ready, and I'll come and pick you up.'

I left her gazing at the graduation photo of Jake.

Colin accompanied me to the door. 'That's terrible news,' I said. 'You and Leonie must be devastated. Thanks for taking the time to talk to Frankie, I know it means a lot to her.'

Colin clapped me on the shoulder. 'No worries, I'm glad she found us. I really wish for Jake's sake it had been sooner. We had a bad experience when we first started foster care — the father of one of our foster kids got out of prison, somehow found out where she was and turned up on our doorstep with a knife, demanding we give her back. So after that, we tightened up our privacy.'

'No-one could blame you for that,' I said. I thought about Frankie and Jake as I drove into the town centre. Would things have turned out differently if she'd found him earlier? Before he'd got into the drugs? Or even after? Maybe she could have helped him to get clean. The worst part was never knowing, you could torture yourself forever with the 'if-onlys' and 'what-ifs' and there were never any answers. Frankie was right.   Closure   was   a   bullshit   word.

Chapter 15

I found a quiet coffee shop in town and worked on my iPad, catching up on emails and organising my work calendar for the next week. Jared had managed to sort out the Bankruptcy Brothers in my absence and they were presenting a united front for court. I couldn't help feeling a bit peeved that he'd been able to achieve what I hadn't.

Frankie messaged me at three o'clock. When I arrived, she opened the front door. Her face was pale and tear-stained, and she was clutching a small cardboard box. Colin and Leonie were standing behind her, and they each gave her a long hug.

'You okay?' I said as we got into the car.

'Yep. They gave me some photos and a couple of Jake's things for keepsakes. They want me to keep in touch and invited me to visit whenever I want. Jake was so lucky to have them for a family. Why the fuck did he have to go and stuff it all up?'

She was bristling with anger. 'I'm so fucking mad at him I could burst. And I'm mad at Tom for leaving him without a Dad. And Mum ... I take it back about not hating her. If she hadn't loved booze more than she loved us, he might have had a fighting chance. Both of us.'

'Yeah, it's tough all right.'

In this situation, words didn't even begin to suffice. I reached over and gave her hand a squeeze.

We were heading towards town. 'What do you want to do now?' I asked. 'Do you want to head home?'

Frankie shrugged. 'I don't know what I want. I want to walk, I want to sleep, I want to get pissed.'

'All right, let's book into a motel for the night and we'll head off first thing tomorrow.'

I found a motel, Avalon Inn, overlooking the ocean and we checked into rooms 24 and 26.

'If you need to talk, I'm right here,' I said to Frankie, as she inserted the key into the front door of her room.

'Thanks. I just need to be alone. Don't worry about dinner, I'll do my own thing.'

A stiff breeze had blown up out of nowhere, but I needed some fresh air; so I put on a jacket and went for a walk along the beach, right round to the marina. I sat on a seat with a view over the bay to the thickly forested shore opposite. The gentle lapping of the water against the boats hypnotised me and I was only dimly aware of the squawking gulls and the flapping of the rigging against the masts of the yachts.

I was back in the motel room with Frankie, holding her in her grief and anger, even though I knew that in reality there was nothing I could do or say that would make any difference.

Dusk was creeping in by the time I got back to the motel. There was no sign of life from Frankie's room and the curtains were drawn. I had dinner by myself in the motel restaurant then went back to my room, picked up my guitar and tried unsuccessfully to work on my new songs. After watching some crap TV, I went to bed at 10 o'clock.

#

I woke up to the sound of hammering on my door. The bedside digital clock said it was 2 am. I pulled on some jocks and opened the door a fraction. 'Who is it?'

'It's me, Frankie.'

I unlatched the door and she fell into my arms. She was sobbing, tidal waves of heaving sobs. I walked her over to my bed and sat her down beside me. I held her for what seemed like forever, her hair soft as clouds against my cheek. The sobs began to ebb. I kissed her neck – it was warm and musky-scented and I kept going up to her delicate ears, her eyebrows, her cheeks and round to her mouth. She responded with a passion that shot through me like an injection of stimulant, and then we were rolling on the bed. Frankie was still in her clothes and as I started to unbutton her shirt, she rolled off the bed, stood up and flung off her clothes.

I rolled off my jocks. After a few perfunctory rubs of my cock – not that it needed any encouragement – she lowered herself on to me and began pumping away, her breasts bobbing rhythmically.

'Wait a minute, ' I said. She stopped. 'Um ... that feels great, but can we slow it down a bit?"

Not that I hadn't had my share of fast and furious in the past, but this was an experience I wanted to savour, down to every last millisecond.

'Fuck, that's a first,' Frankie said.

'What is? Being asked to slow down?'

'Usually it's just wham-bam-thank-you-ma'am. And forget the thank-you.'

I assumed she was referring to Eddie. So he wasn't so hot in bed. Why didn't that surprise me?

I reached up and stroked a tendril of hair away from her face. In the moonlight shining through the bedroom curtain she was a ghostly silhouette.

'You don't have to put up with that, you know.'

'What is this, sex therapy?'

She heaved herself off me. My cock flopped out, shrunk and dejected.

'The trouble with you, Will, is that you're always in your head, thinking and analysing. You can never just let go and enjoy yourself.'

She got off the bed, turned on the bedside lamp and began picking her clothes up from the floor.

'Please don't go. If you don't want to make love, that's fine. It will just be nice sleeping with you.'

'Another first.' But there was a smile in her voice. She draped her clothes over the couch then got back into bed, turned her back and I draped my arm over her and pulled her close to me. Her body curved into mine. Within seconds I could hear her steady breathing; but I stayed awake, trying to still the million thoughts racing around in my mind. Maybe Frankie was right, maybe I did think too much. But how could I help it? I was a lawyer. I was paid to think.

The rattle of a breakfast tray being delivered next door woke me up. I checked the time. 8.05. I didn't remember drifting off. Frankie started to stir. I ran my hands over her body, feeling and exploring every inch, then did the same with my lips. She was still and silent to begin with, but her nipples hardened and her breathing became ragged. My tongue flicked and dipped and twisted and when she came, gasping, I entered her and started the slow dance all over again. She cried out and that made me come, and then we lay in each other's arms in that half-awake, half-asleep post-coital bliss, until the room cleaner rapped on our door at 10 o'clock.

Chapter 16

Frankie was silent as we sped along the highway back to Sydney. She was pale, and her eyes were puffy and red from all the crying of the previous night. Our lovemaking had been a complete surprise to me. Not that I hadn't wanted it; I'd never dreamed it would happen. From the way Frankie had responded, I knew it was more than just physical. If it wasn't, she was a better actor than I gave her credit for. Whatever her response, I had to tell her.

'About last night. I just want you to know it wasn't just a one night stand. For me, anyway.'

'It has to be. I'm with Eddie, remember?'

'He's in jail for at least the next 12 months, maybe longer.'

'So what are you suggesting? That I have an affair with you while he's in jail?'

I'm suggesting you ditch him altogether. But somehow, I didn't think that would go down well.

'So you're just going to put your life on hold while he's in jail?'

'What choice do I have?'

I didn't answer. I felt her eyes on me.

'Look, I know you think he's just another criminal, and I admit he's done some bad things, but deep down he's a good person.'

I bet that's what Jack the Ripper's victims thought, just before he hacked them to pieces.

'I know of lots of guys whose girlfriends play up while they're inside and sometimes they come home to find a kid that's not theirs. That's not going to happen to Eddie; I'm going to be there for him when he gets out. We want to start a family and I think being a father will be really good for him."

Was she trying to convince herself as well as me? I didn't share her faith in Eddie's deep down goodness, but I kept my mouth shut. Anything I said would just sound like sour grapes from a thwarted lover – which they were.

We were halfway to Sydney when Frankie said, 'Can I drive? I've never driven an Audi.'

I hesitated. I had never let anyone drive my car, not even Steph when her car was at the repairer's. I'd insisted on driving her.

'I can show you my driver's licence, Mr Law and Order.'

'No need for that. I'll find a spot to pull over.'

A couple of kilometres down the road there was a truck rest stop. I pulled over and got out, handing her the keys. It was on the tip of my tongue to say 'For God's sake, be careful!' but I refrained. It was a pointless thing to say anyway – very few people get into a car with the deliberate intention of driving recklessly and smashing themselves and the car up.

Frankie pulled out onto the road and put her foot down. A couple of times, the speedometer crept over 110 kilometres an hour, and she glanced at me and grinned. 'Chill out, I know what I'm doing. I learned to drive on dodgem cars, remember?'

'That's what I'm afraid of.'

She was calm and controlled as she sat at the wheel, with her hands in the exact ten-to-two position that I never seemed to achieve. As we approached the outskirts of Sydney, I asked, 'Do you want me to take over?'

'No way, I'm having too much fun. This car is sensational to drive.' She glanced at me. 'Can you stand the stress?"

'No stress, I'm enjoying being chauffeur-driven,' I lied.

I'd planned to drop Frankie off at Central Station so she could catch a train home. Once we got into the city traffic, she really turned on the driving, like something out of Top Gear – adroitly negotiating the traffic, weaving in and out to get ahead, knowing exactly when to brake and when to accelerate. A half-smile hovered around her lips as she tapped her foot to U2 playing on the car stereo.

Then in a moment of clarity, I knew. 'You drove the getaway car for the robbery, didn't you?'

'Are you asking me as a lawyer or a friend?'

'I'm asking you as someone who's made love to you even though you have a boyfriend and didn't regret one second of it.'

'You already know the answer then.'

'Why?'

She kept her gaze on the road as she slowed down for a red light. 'If it wasn't me, it would be someone else and that someone would probably be a shitty driver.'

'Did you know Eddie had a gun?'

'Yes.'

'So you knowingly took part in an armed robbery, fully aware that Eddie had a gun and could have hurt or killed someone?'

I was surprised at the vehemence of the anger that shook my voice. Frankie's grip on the steering wheel tightened until her knuckles were white. A line of tears tracked down her face. If she was trying to pull the sympathy card, it wasn't working.

'He had me in a headlock with a knife,' she said dully. 'He told me if I didn't agree to help him, he'd slit my throat.'

'And this is the man who's a good person deep down and is going to be a good father to your kids? Jesus, Frankie, what planet are you living on?'

'It's the drugs – when he's clean he's a different person...' Her voice trailed off.

'How many more times will he threaten you before he gives up the drugs, if he ever does? Next time he might kill you.'

Frankie swerved into the left lane, narrowly missing a Jeep, which blared its horn at her, and then pulled into a delivery parking space outside an office block. She reached over, hauled her overnight bag out from the back seat and handed me the keys.

'Listen, Mr Up-Yourself-Goody-Two-Shoes lawyer, just because you fucked me doesn't give you the right to tell me how to run my life. You know nothing about Eddie, or me. Go back to your mansion on the beach, and your snobby family and your whingeing, filthy rich clients, and leave me alone.'

She opened the car door and sprang out.

'Frankie, wait!'

She slammed the car door and crossed the road, dodging the traffic, her overnight bag bobbing against her shoulder. I watched her until she disappeared into the crowd.

#

I stopped off at my apartment, changed into my work clothes and went into the office. My desk was a mess of papers, but I couldn't get motivated to make a start. Louis poked his head through the door.

'Back a day early! Did you get sick of the family?'

'Two days is about one-and-a-half days too long.'

He grinned. 'I know what you mean. A few of us are going to Players after work for a couple of drinks. Want to come?'

Players was a restaurant and nightclub, the type of place where businessmen went for after-work drinks, and often stayed until the early hours of the morning. I was about to decline, not being in the mood for socialising, but decided it might be better than sitting at home thinking about Frankie.

But as I sat on a velveteen couch in the lounge bar, bathed in blue and purple light with Shakira belting it out in the background and listening to the partners discussing the ups and downs of the Sydney property market, I wished I'd gone with my first impulse to go home. The two paralegals, Emma and Rose, were discussing Rose's upcoming $50,000 wedding, and Jared and the other graduate lawyer, Bryce, were sitting at the bar, a good vantage point for checking out the women.

I felt a strange sense of disconnection from them all, as if I were watching their lives through a window – lives that were completely foreign to me. And yet it was only three months ago that I'd sat in this same club, and drank and cracked jokes with them until we'd been asked by the manager very politely (then not so politely) to leave.

I slipped out at 9.30 before anyone could make a big deal of my leaving early while still stone cold sober. I'd left my car at work, so I caught a cab home. A brackish wind whipped around me as I got out. Although the spring days were clear and balmy, the nights reminded you that winter wasn't yet ready to relinquish its hold. As I entered my apartment block foyer, I was instantly enveloped in its warmth. I walked up the two flights of stairs to my apartment, dug my keys out of my pocket and felt in the darkness for the shape of my front door key. Something whacked me on the head and it exploded with pain. Then nothing.

Chapter 17

11 months later. September 2007

You're so tough on the outside

But you're just a little girl wanting to hide

Your eyes tell a story of sorrow and pain

But darling when I see you again

There'll be no past

Just today.

A table of girls on a hen's night out at The Three Monkeys clapped and whistled as I faded out of the song 'Just Today'. It was the missing song on my album, the one I'd struggled with for so long. It had come to me, fully formed, after I'd recovered from my blow to the head, as if it had been waiting there all along for me to find it and transpose it.

'Thanks everyone, just taking a small break,' I said into the microphone, 'Don't go away, I'll be back soon.'

A young couple wandered over to the side of the stage where I had copies of my CD for sale on a table. The girl picked up the CD cover. *Life's a Stage – Will McPherson*. I still felt a glow of pride six months after its release. This was something tangible I'd created from my own mind, which now had a life of its own. Sales had been pretty good for an indie album by an unknown; but even if it touched only a few people, it seemed more significant than being an expert on bankruptcy, or any facet of the law. There were countless lawyers who could do the same job as me, with the same level of expertise, but there was only one Will McPherson who could write these songs.

'I loved that last song,' the girl said. 'It made me cry.'

Her boyfriend rolled his eyes at me, but I ignored him. I smiled at the girl.

'Thanks, it's one of my favourites too.' I was on her side. I wanted her to buy the CD, which she did.

I sat at the bar, sipping my mineral water. I'd had a lot of people compliment me on that song, which I secretly called Frankie's Song. It was without a doubt the best song on the album. It was probably just as well she'd never heard it; it would just give her a chance to reject me again and twist the knife even further.

I'd had no contact with her since the attack on me almost 12 months ago. Not that I hadn't tried, despite the warning in the crumpled note that I found shoved under the front door after I came to – 'Stay away from Eddie's missus. Next time you won't wake up'.

I'd phoned Frankie numerous times and left text messages. I even phoned Mrs Magic Cleaning and left messages for her to phone me. All to no avail. The police investigated the matter but said they had no leads and advised me that the best course of action was, as the note said, to stay away from Eddie's missus. I wondered if she'd been attacked as well and that was why she hadn't responded to my messages; and each time, I felt a stab of guilt that I was responsible. I was in a state of constant flux – wanting to see her again but not wanting to endanger her safety.

Joe jolted me out of my thoughts. 'Good night, mate?'

'Pretty good, the 50th birthday crowd is pretty keen. Looks like I'll be doing plenty of Eagles and Rolling Stones later on.'

I felt a hand on my shoulder. I turned around and looked straight into those beautiful, haunted eyes.

'Hi,' Frankie said. Her smile was uncertain, as if unsure of her reception.

My words stuck in my throat. My first thought was that my psychic powers had summoned her – I'd been thinking of her and there she was. Even though I didn't believe in psychic powers. God how I'd missed her. She was standing two feet away from me, yet I was acutely aware of every inch of her, right down to the beating of her heart and the blood pumping through her veins.

'Hi, stranger,' I finally said.

'I heard your last song,' she said.

My embarrassment was overlaid by surprise. 'Where were you sitting? I didn't see you.'

She pointed in a vague direction behind me. 'Over there, behind the post.' She was wearing orange jeans, boots and a purple velvet jacket over a snug jumper that moulded her breasts. *Don't look at her breasts.*

'Was it about me?'

I nodded. Her eyes grew misty. 'I've never had a song written about me before.'

'It's about you and it's for you. It's yours to keep forever. If I'd known you were coming, I'd have wrapped it up with a bow and presented it to you.'

She gave a wistful smile that made my heart turn over.

'So you just happened to be in the area?'

'I came by to apologise. About you being attacked.'

'It's a bit late now.' I took her hand. 'Sorry, I didn't mean to snap at you. I was pretty pissed off at the time, not to mention sore, but there was no permanent damage. I was more concerned about you.'

'I got a note saying you'd been done over and if I had any more contact with you, they'd do me over too.'

'I got a threatening note as well. Just in case knocking me unconscious wasn't enough.'

Frankie stared at her feet. 'Yeah, I'm sorry.'

'Stop apologising – it's not your fault.'

'Two days afterwards I got a big bunch of flowers delivered, and a note from Eddie saying he was sorry for threatening me.'

'So that made everything right again?'

She looked daggers at me, but before she could answer, Joe interrupted.

'Would the lady like a drink?'

'No thanks,' Frankie said.

'You're taking a risk coming here tonight then,' I said.

'He's backed off now; he gets out on parole in a couple of weeks. That's the other reason I came – to say goodbye.'

Of course. I should have seen that coming.

'Where are you going?' I tried to sound casual, as if my hopes hadn't been built up and dashed to pieces in the space of a few minutes.

'Maitland. No-one knows us there and we can make a fresh start. Eddie's already got a labouring job lined up and I'll get work, I don't care what I do.'

What could I say? Have a good life?

'Frankie, I want to ask you something. Will you promise to answer me honestly?'

'I'm not promising anything till I hear the question.'

'What hold has Eddie got over you?'

'What do you mean?'

'You're an intelligent, gorgeous woman. And you've got guts. If you wanted out of that relationship, you'd just get up and go. Violence or no violence. There are plenty of people who can help you. So there must be a reason you're hanging in.'

"I love him.'

'Can you look me in the eye and tell me that?'

She held my gaze but said nothing.

'Or is it fear?'

She looked over my shoulder and signalled to Joe. 'I've changed my mind. I'll have a rum and Coke, please.'

She refused to let me pay for it. After Joe delivered it, she took a sip then swirled the ice around in her glass with her straw. 'Eddie's changed. I can see it when I visit him. He's been going to counselling in prison and he's determined to stay straight, for the sake of our future family. When he's not on drugs, he's the sweetest guy.'

I had a major problem with the words 'Eddie and 'sweetest' being linked together, but I swallowed my revulsion. I checked my watch. I should have been back on stage five minutes ago.

'Can you hang around for a while? I'll be finished in an hour. I'll buy you another drink.'

'I don't think...'

'You owe me – it's the least you can do after me spending a night in hospital and walking around with a huge egg on my head, which gave rise to all sorts of unsavoury speculation.'

She gave me one of her looks. 'You really know how to play dirty. First you tell me it wasn't my fault, then you pull out the guilt card to bribe me into having a drink with you.'

I grinned. 'What do you expect from a lawyer? As far as I'm concerned, the end justifies the means.'

She sighed. 'Okay, just one drink.'

She took her glass and perched on a nearby stool. The birthday group welcomed me back exuberantly and as predicted, inundated me with requests for covers from the 70s and 80s. I felt Frankie's eyes on me, and I played and sang harder and stronger, softer and more expressively than I ever had before, as if all the songs had been created from my own inner core.

A couple of songs in I noticed Sarah at the bar, talking to the bar manager and watching me at the same time. I hadn't seen her all night as she'd been supervising in the function room upstairs. I flashed her a smile and she waved back.

I finished an Eagles bracket then a male voice yelled, 'Play "Brown Eyed Girl" again!'

'I think once a night for "Brown-Eyed Girl" is enough,' I replied, to raucous laughter. 'But I can do another Van Morrison song called "Someone Like You." It's a beautiful song and there's a beautiful lady sitting in the audience who can sing it with me. Come on up, Frankie!'

Everyone swivelled around and Frankie glared at me with laser-like intensity. A chant started up to the rhythm of clapping hands: 'Frankie! Frankie!'

'Come on, Frankie!' I called. 'They love you already and you haven't even sung a note!'

Crowd expectation exerts powerful pressure; but even so, I half expected Frankie to get up and walk out. But she made her way to the stage, accompanied by cheers and whistles.

'You arsehole!' she hissed at me.

'You can thank me later.' Someone handed me up another chair and I plugged in the second mike, which I always carried with me. I placed the sheet music on the music stand. 'You know this song?'

'Too bad if I don't, isn't it?'

I wasn't perturbed, as I knew she'd pick it up quickly. I sang the first verse, which gave her time to familiarise herself with the melody, then she sang the second verse. Her honeyed tones dipped and soared effortlessly and imbued the song with such an undertone of bitter-sweetness that a lump rose in my throat. As we came to the final chorus, I suddenly became aware of my surroundings – of the stillness in the audience, and the throng of faces all turned towards us.

The final notes faded away to thunderous applause and whistles. 'More! More! Moondance!'

I raised my eyebrows at Frankie. She shrugged, which I took for a 'yes,' so we launched into 'Moondance', followed by the classic favourite, 'Eagle Rock'. By now the dance floor was packed, bodies in various stages of intoxication bouncing and shuffling. After a few more dance songs and a second rendition of Happy Birthday for the birthday boy, who was by now looking the worse for wear and decidedly older than his 50 years, we wound it up. The crowd started to fizzle out and the hard-core partygoers stayed on the dance floor bopping to the jukebox.

Frankie went to find us a table while I ordered us a drink at the bar.

'That was great,' a voice said at my shoulder.

I turned around. Sarah was smiling at me. 'Your friend was fantastic. Was that really an impromptu performance?'

'Yes. Frankie's got the knack of being able to hear a melody and harmonise perfectly first time.'

'Have you two known each other long?'

'Not really. I met her briefly at a pub where she was doing a gig; so when I saw her here tonight, I called her up on stage. I knew she'd be brilliant.'

I was surprised at how easily that lie had presented itself to me and how glibly I told it. Admittedly, I'd had lots of practice recently. At the same time I was annoyed with myself for feeling compelled to lie to Sarah. What did it matter what she thought of my relationship with Frankie? The fact that she wanted more than friendship from me was surely her problem, not mine.

Joe handed me my drinks and before Sarah had time to probe further, I said, 'Gotta go. See you next time'.

I found Frankie at a corner table and as I sat down, I said, 'You're a natural. I've told you this before – you should be doing this as a career.'

'Yeah, right.'

Her offhand comment was belied by the glow on her face. I'd watched her face as she sang, luminescent with the joy of a wanderer who'd found home, a place where she belonged. This was where she was meant to be – singing. With me. The two of us. How could I convince her?

'Seriously, Frankie, you could have sung a page out of the telephone directory and they'd have loved it. You made it sound as if we sing together all the time.'

She shrugged. 'I enjoy it, but it's not something that brings in a steady wage.'

'I guess Eddie wouldn't be too happy about it. You up on stage, the centre of attention, all the men ogling you.'

Her face closed over. I'd broken the spell. Dammit – why did I have to spoil it by bringing up Eddie?

I stroked her hand. 'Sorry, let's change the subject. Will you spend the night with me?'

She looked away. But I'd seen it in her eyes – a desire so naked my heart skipped a beat.

'What's the point?' she said dully.

'I want to spend a night with you while I have the opportunity. Who knows if we'll get another chance?'

What the hell, I had nothing to lose. She was going off to play happy families with Eddie and I'd already bared my soul to her in my song.

'In case you haven't guessed, I'm in love with you, Frankie. There hasn't been a minute in the last few months you haven't been on my mind. You've chosen to be with Eddie and I'm not going to pretend I'm okay with that, but I also know there's nothing I can do about it. So let's forget about all that and just enjoy being together tonight.'

Frankie took a deep breath. "Okay, on one condition. That we don't go to your place. I don't want to take any chances.'

'Okay, I'll book us into a motel. There's one just down the road.'

'And another condition. That you don't mention the word love.'

#

The motel room was less than ideal for a last romantic tryst. Cheerless décor, faded curtains and scratched bedside tables. The Air Wick air freshener was fighting a losing battle with the musty odour. I'd bought a bottle of champagne from the bottle shop before we left the hotel and we sat up in bed, propped up by the lumpy pillows and sipped it out of chipped wine glasses.

I put my glass down, gently removed Frankie's glass from her hand, tilted her face towards me and kissed her. I felt her defences dissolving as surely as if she were in a flotation tank. Our lovemaking was an opera of sighing, whispering, moaning, gasping, with both of us playing all the roles. My passion was so overwhelming that I had to consciously rein myself in, for fear of hurting Frankie. She responded with an intensity sparked by the desperation of knowing this was the last time we'd be together.

Afterwards as Frankie lay in my arms, I watched the dancing patterns the car lights made on the curtains. I was tired, the sublime tiredness of total repletion, but I couldn't allow myself to fall asleep. I wanted to cherish every last second.

'If money were no object, what would you want most in the world?' I asked.

Frankie ran her fingers through my chest hair. 'Money can't buy what I want most in the world.'

I waited for her to continue.

'All I want is a family. People make fun of wanting the cottage in a small town with the white picket fence but that's exactly what I want. Mum and Dad cuddling on the couch, kids kicking a ball in the backyard, a roast cooking in the oven. And the kids knowing that their parents will always be there for them and that they'd kill anyone who tried to take them away. It probably sounds boring to you but that's my dream.'

'I think it's a beautiful dream.' I traced my finger around her ear. 'You could have that dream with me.'

Frankie drew in a long breath that sounded like a half-sob. 'I can't. It's too late.'

It's never too late. I wish you could see that.

I drew her into me so closely I could feel her heart beating against my chest. I soon heard her steady, rhythmic breathing and fell into a deep dreamless sleep, the best I'd had in the last 12 months.

Chapter 18

Six years later. August 2013

Maria Catalano leaned back in her sumptuous leather office chair and surveyed me.

'So, Mr McPherson, why are you here?'

'My wife wanted me to come. Insisted, really.'

Maria flashed me a curt smile. 'If I had a dollar for every time I heard that from a client, I could retire. Why did she insist that you come?'

'I've been a bit hard to live with lately. Snappy, irritable, some days it's a huge effort just to get out of bed. And I'm not sleeping well. I don't know why – maybe I'm having an early midlife crisis. I told Sarah I'm sure it will pass, but she said three months is long enough and I should see someone.'

'Was there something that happened three months ago that may have triggered those feelings?'

'My sister was involved in a bad accident in America and she was in a coma. It was touch and go for a while. I flew over when it happened – the whole family did.'

The memory of Steph in hospital still made my heart lurch – bandaged, tubes hanging out of her, she looked like an alien creature. She'd finished her exercise physiology degree, married an American, and was living and working in

Chicago. As she was riding her bike at dawn along a Chicago city street, training for a triathlon, a truck took a corner too quickly and barrelled her over.

'That must have been a terrible shock.'

Maria's reply was warm and empathic, but I got the impression she was finding an extra dimension in my words that I had no idea about.

'It was.' The shock of the phone call from her husband Mark, the rush to organise time off work and buy plane tickets, the agonisingly long flight over there, the two weeks spent by Steph's side in hospital until she came out of her coma. It was all a blurry nightmare.

'But fortunately, she pulled through the coma. She amazed the doctors; she's one tough lady. She's got no permanent brain damage thank goodness, but she's got a lot of therapy ahead of her before she can walk again. She flew home a couple of weeks ago and she's staying with our parents to recuperate.'

Mum had taken on a new lease of life, making Steph's rehabilitation her major project. Protein smoothies, physiotherapist appointments, fit balls and other exercise paraphernalia taking over the house. I guessed she found it more fulfilling than attending fundraising events for war orphans, worthy though that was. Particularly as Mark decided he couldn't handle Steph's incapacitation, packed his bags and disappeared.

'Events like that affect people in different ways,' Maria said. 'All those symptoms you described could be your body's response to shock.'

'Really? I admit at first it was scary when we thought she might die, but she's been out of critical care for weeks. Why would I still be feeling the shock now?'

'It may be taking you longer to process it. However, there could be another reason.'

She scribbled something on her notebook then looked up. 'If you've had a shock in the past that you haven't dealt with or resolved, it will be lurking there in your subconscious and every subsequent shock you have will bring up memories of that incident. So, in effect, you experience a double whammy of shock."

She looked at me keenly. 'Could that be the case with you?'

I considered it. 'I don't think so.'

'You may have to think about it, as it could be an experience you've dismissed as not being important.'

'The only thing I can think of is that I was in a shop when it was held up and the guy threatened me with a gun. But that was eight years ago and it was all over in less than two minutes. It was a shock at the time, but I was okay afterwards.'

'Did you get counselling for it? Or talk to anyone about it?'

'Not really, apart from the police. They gave me the number of a victims' counselling service but I didn't take it up. I didn't feel the need for it.'

'Being a victim of an armed hold-up is a traumatic experience. I don't think anybody could come out of that without some emotional impact. And men in particular often cover it up and convince themselves they're okay, because despite our so-called enlightened society, it's often still considered taboo for them to admit they're scared.'

'I have no trouble admitting I'm scared when the situation arises,' I snapped. 'And of course I was scared. Who wouldn't be, with a gun waved in their face? But there's no point raking it up again now.'

'All right.' She had a calm, serene presence about her. I had a feeling that if I'd admitted to murder, it wouldn't have fazed her. She shuffled some papers on her desk and handed me a few sheets. 'Here are some questions I'd like you to answer. They help me gauge if there are any issues with anxiety and depression, and how you're coping with life in general.'

After I'd answered so many multiple choice questions about my thoughts, emotions and actions that my head was spinning, Maria said, 'That's all for today. I'll analyse the results and discuss them with you at your next appointment.'

She smiled. 'I assume there will be a next appointment?'

I shrugged. 'I guess. I have to find out if I'm crazy or not.'

As I opened the door she said, 'I'd really like you to think about what I said. About whether the impact of the hold-up could be affecting you now.'

#

'So, what was Maria like? Was she easy to talk to?'

I kept my eyes fixed on the road ahead of me. Sarah had already asked me twice, in different ways, how the session had gone.

'We didn't do a lot of talking – I had to answer a lot of questions that apparently indicate whether I'm anxious or depressed and we're going to discuss those next time.'

We were both silent as I negotiated my way through the late afternoon traffic to my parents' house at Woollahra. It was an awkward silence – I knew Sarah was dying to ask more about the session but didn't want to upset me. And I didn't want to talk about it. But she was my wife and I should want to talk to her. And she had put up with my moods.

'She thinks that the shock of Steph's accident could have triggered memories of the hold-up and resulted in a sort of delayed after-shock.'

'That's interesting. What do you think?'

'I think it all sounds a bit far-fetched. I'm a bit wary of this deep, subconscious stuff when often there's a really simple explanation for how someone is behaving.'

'Maybe you shouldn't discount it without at least giving it some thought.'

I glanced at her. She'd slimmed down since we'd married and had her blonde hair cut and bobbed, which suited her role as public relations manager of the Corporate City hotel group – a big step up from assistant manager of The Three Monkeys. Her face, now thinner and sharper, looked drawn.

I squeezed her knee. 'I have been known to be wrong. I promise I'll give it some serious consideration.'

She smiled and squeezed my hand back. I told myself I was lucky she thought the world of me and had agreed to marry me. I'd buy her a bunch of flowers tomorrow and take her to our favourite Thai restaurant. Better still, I'd take her away for the weekend to a secluded coastal resort, where we could frolic on the beach, drink cocktails and make love. Although sex had become imbued with all sorts of undertones, now that we'd been trying for almost a year to have a baby.

Mum gave us the usual effusive welcome. Sarah had charmed all my family – even my father, who was not easily given to praise, had declared, 'She's got beauty and brains. Count yourself very lucky, my boy.' The subtext was clear – I didn't deserve her and it was nothing short of a miracle that she'd married me.

Steph was in the living room watching TV. My heart squeezed every time I saw her – my healthy, full-of-life sister reduced to a pale shell of herself, shrunken into the wheelchair as if it was a natural extension of her body.

'So it's come down to watching "The Bold and the Beautiful",' I said. 'Want me to get your slippers and warm milk?'

Steph picked up a cushion from the nearby couch and threw it at me. The good thing was you soon forgot about her injury – her spirit shone out larger than her body. She was determined to not only walk again, despite the doctors' doubts, but to run another triathlon.

'How good will this be for my career?' she'd said recently. 'Now that I know what it's like recovering from chronic injuries, I'll have real empathy for my clients.'

I'd witnessed her in some dark moods, so I was happy to see her natural optimism brimming up again. Mum brought in a tray of coffee and muffins, and a protein shake for Steph. Dad was at a meeting at the University, which was a relief. One less loaded comment about my change of career to contend with.

'You look tired,' Mum said to Sarah. 'You're working too hard.'

She gave me an accusing glance, as if it were my fault. In my parents' eyes, it was bad enough that I'd given up a well-paid, high-status career for a modestly-paid job as a financial counsellor with Debt Solutions, a not-for-profit community organisation; but the fact that my wife earned twice my salary and was the main breadwinner was something they couldn't accept. It upset the natural order of things.

'It's been pretty full-on lately,' Sarah said, 'I'm hoping to have a break soon.'

'I was thinking of taking you away this weekend,' I said. 'A nice, quiet beach where we can get away from everything."

'I have to go to a conference on Saturday; it's for all the executive staff. I told you about it.'

You idiot, you should have checked with her before blurting it out.

There was a knock on the front door followed by a 'Hullo!' The door opened.

'Come on, Cooper. Amelia, pick up your teddy please."

'Oh, that's Nick and Jaclyn,' Mum said unnecessarily. 'They're going to a law society function tonight so they're dropping the kids off.'

Nick bowled into the living room leading five-year-old Amelia by the hand and with three-year-old Cooper in his arms. Jaclyn was behind him holding an overflowing zip-up bag with a box of Lego perched on top. She looked sporty-glamorous in sweat pants and halterneck top, her hair in a ponytail. She was back in the gym two months after the birth of each child.

'How is everyone?' Nick asked, without waiting for an answer. 'The traffic over was horrendous. Kids, go and give Grandma a hug.'

Amelia rushed over to Mum, who scooped her up in her arms. Cooper clung to his father, regarding Mum with a terrified look, as if she were about to eat him.

'He's such a Daddy's boy,' Nick said. "Never mind, Coop, I'll tell Grandma that you counted to 20 all by yourself this morning.'

'Oh, that's wonderful, Cooper,' Mum cooed. 'What a clever boy you are.'

If I found Nick hard to take before, he was insufferable since he'd become a father, recounting every little milestone of his children as if they were child prodigies. After a ten-minute discourse on Amelia's superior skills in university-level maths for pre-schoolers, Nick turned to me.

'By the way, did you know your Mr Gisbourne has got himself in trouble again?'

I tensed. 'What's he done?'

'He was convicted of assault. A colleague of mine was in the same court on another matter. The victim was his girlfriend. He got a suspended sentence – should have served time, if you ask me. Apparently his lawyer spouted some bullshit that he'd finished his parole successfully, and this was an aberration and he was going to anger management counselling, and the magistrate obviously swallowed it. Getting through parole without a black mark proves nothing – it just means he wasn't caught.'

Frankie was my first thought. What had he done to her? She sprang to life in my mind's eye, with a black eye and split lip. Or was it worse? Broken bones? I felt the heat of anger rising up inside me.

'So he's back in Sydney?' I asked.

'It was in Burwood Local Court. I didn't know that he'd left Sydney. Or that you were keeping track of his movements.'

I felt Sarah's questioning look. I shrugged. 'Someone told me he'd left town. And I felt relieved at the time because there was less chance that our paths would cross.'

Mum's brow creased. 'I've been afraid all along that he'd seek you out and do something terrible to you. In revenge.'

'Logically, he doesn't have grounds for revenge. He pleaded guilty so I didn't have to give evidence. He's the one in the wrong. But logic doesn't count for those guys.'

'I wouldn't worry about it,' Nick said. 'It's been what … seven or eight years? His only concern will be how he's getting his next supply of drugs. He'll have forgotten you well and truly."

Somehow I doubted it. And I certainly hadn't forgotten him.

Chapter 19

In the car on the way home, Sarah said, 'Are you really worried about that Gisbourne character being back in town?'

I shook my head. 'Nick's right. It's been a long time. If he was going to do anything to me, he would have done it by now.'

I hadn't told anyone about the assault on me after Frankie and I had returned from our trip, apart from the police. I'd explained the lump on my head by saying I was mugged late at night in the city while waiting for a taxi. It would have been impossible to explain without divulging my relationship with Frankie, which I didn't want to do. Not even to Sarah. Especially not to Sarah. I told myself it was none of her business, it happened before we started our relationship; but the reality was that my relationship with Frankie was difficult to talk about and I wasn't sure she'd understand. Hell, I didn't understand it myself.

I tossed and turned all night into the early hours of the morning. The more I tried to blot Frankie out of my mind, the more she popped up; so real I could almost believe it was her steady breathing I could hear beside me instead of Sarah's. She'd always been there in the back of my mind; and when I allowed myself the luxury of thinking about her, I wondered what she was doing right at that moment, and if she was thinking of me. I sent my thoughts winging through space to her and imagined her catching them at the other end.

But now there was another image of her that wouldn't leave me – a battered, bruised, defeated Frankie. On the last occasion we were together, she was convinced that Eddie had cleaned up his act and that a bright new future awaited them. I remembered the information from his sentencing, that he had two previous convictions for domestic violence, which I had later figured out were committed during his relationship with Frankie.

It was clear now that he hadn't changed and never would. I was as certain of that as I'd been of anything in my life.

#

By the time I got up and stumbled into the shower, I'd come to a decision. I had to see Frankie again, just to make sure she was okay. As a friend, it was my obligation to help her – the very least I could do was try and persuade her to leave Eddie, and start the new life she deserved.

The dilemma was how to arrange it. Assuming she still had the same contact details, I could either send her an email or text message; but I couldn't be sure that Eddie wasn't checking her phone. I'd bite the bullet and ring her from my work phone, so the number wouldn't be identified as mine.

When I arrived at work, my first clients were already waiting for me – a couple in their forties who were up to their eyeballs in debt after the husband had lost his job. A common scenario but as was usually the case, they'd left it until the bailiffs were beating down the door before getting help. We discussed a plan to contact creditors and arrange payment plans for each of them.

'It doesn't help that Harry guzzles a six-pack every night,' Alice, his wife said. 'That's money down the drain we could be using to pay off our debts.'

'Quit your nagging,' Harry said. 'Drinking is the only pleasure I have left in life. Take that away and I may as well...' He made the gesture of slitting his throat.

Being a financial counsellor usually meant counselling in other areas of life as well, as lack of money impacts on everything. I'd managed to score the job without any formal counselling qualifications, and I was straightforward and practical in my approach. If my clients had serious problems such as gambling or substance abuse, I referred them to specialist agencies.

'At your next appointment, we'll do a detailed budget,' I said, handing them their appointment card. 'And Harry, just a heads-up, you'll need to drastically reduce your drinking if you're going to get yourself out of this mess. It's your choice – drinking or being debt-free.'

Alice gave a triumphant smile as they left, with Harry muttering under his breath.

'Another happy customer,' smiled my boss Delia, a plump, middle-aged woman who exuded motherly common sense.

When she left to attend a meeting, I shut the door of my office and picked up the phone. Before I could talk myself out of it, I dialled the number. After a few rings, I was about to hang up when a breathless voice said, 'Hullo?'

This is not a good idea. Hang up now. I ignored the warning voice in my head.

'Frankie, it's Will. Please don't hang up.'

Silence.

'Are you alone?' I asked.

'I'm at the shops. But yes, I'm alone.'

What do you say after so long? The six years since I'd last seen Frankie seemed a lifetime ago.

'How are you?'

'I'm fine.' Her tone was guarded. 'Why are you ringing?'

'I heard that Eddie was in court recently. For an assault on you.'

'Yeah.' There was a defiant tone to her voice, the implication being, 'So, what's it to you?'

'I just wondered how you were. Obviously things aren't good at the moment.'

'What gives you the right after all these years to ring up out of the blue and make assumptions about my personal life, which you know nothing about?'

'I know I have no right at all. Except that of someone who's concerned about you. I care about you, Frankie, there's no time limit to that."

'That's very touching, but I don't need your concern. Find someone who does.'

She hung up. I kind of expected that response. Maybe I deserved it. Because I was kidding myself if I thought my motives for getting in contact with her were purely out of friendship. That much was clear as soon as I heard her voice.

Chapter 20

According to the psychological tests that Maria ran, I scored high on anxiety and moderately high on depression.

'That's pretty normal for someone dealing with psychological trauma,' she said at the beginning of our second session. 'What we need to determine now is what you want to get out of these sessions.'

'My only goal is to find a way of disposing of Edward Gisbourne, a giant carbuncle on the face of humanity.'

Maria raised her eyebrows. 'What brought this on?'

I told her about Gisbourne ostensibly being back in town and about his recent conviction. As I had no desire to go into my relationship with Frankie, I ended with, 'So, he's not only a bank robber but he beats his wife up as well. That's the lowest of low, as far as I'm concerned.'

'What exactly did he do?'

'I don't know the details. But knowing him, it wouldn't be a clout around the ear. He'd make a good job of it.'

'What was there about him that makes you think that?'

'He's got a real air of menace about him – and I don't think it's just because he pointed a gun at me. I could sense it in court – he'd beat you up if you so much as looked at him the wrong way.'

Maria continued her gently persistent questioning; and before I realised what I was doing, I was recounting the events of the night of the hold-up. It was amazing how many details I'd forgotten. The dull grey metal of the gun. The eyes staring at me through the stocking. The swish of car tyres on the wet road outside. The loud ker-ching as Mike opened the cash register. My body – numb on the outside, but quaking on the inside. How two minutes had seemed like two hours.

By the time I'd finished talking my chest was burning. In my mind's eye I was beating the crap out of Eddie, blow after blow until he was a bloody, bone-shattered mess writhing on the floor.

'What are you feeling right at this moment?' Maria asked me.

'What do you think?'

'I could take a guess but I want you to tell me.'

'For God's sake, this is kindergarten stuff. You want me to finger paint it?'

I got up and strode out.

#

Maria had given me some literature on dealing with trauma, with particular reference to victims of crime. It included information on how to cope with anger, suggesting talking to a counsellor or friend, going for a walk or jog, or punching a boxing bag. I didn't do any of those things. I headed straight for the pub.

It was the nearest pub to Maria's office, the sort I would never go to normally, frequented by tradies and labourers – sweat and plaster dust mingling with the stale, beer-soaked carpet. Under the comforting cover of rough chat and raucous laughter, I drank myself into oblivion then caught a cab home, staggering through the front door at ten o'clock to a tight-lipped Sarah. She refrained from saying anything and I knew it was because she was trying to be understanding, but it irritated me even more and I swatted away her attempts to help me undress and get into bed.

Maria rang me the next day, concerned about my well-being after my angry exit from our session. I was sitting at my desk nursing a throbbing hangover.

'I'm fine,' I said. 'And I'm sorry I stormed out.'

'No need to apologise,' Maria said. 'I know it was painful for you reliving it again, but often just the act of talking about it relieves a lot of the tension and the stress. Like pricking a boil and letting all the pus out.'

I grimaced. As my stomach was also feeling delicate, this imagery was doing nothing to help my recovery.

'Now that we've started the process,' she continued, 'it's important that we keep going so you can process all your thoughts and feelings and come to some resolution. Do you want to schedule another appointment now?'

'Er ... I've got to rush off to a meeting. I'll get back to you.'

I didn't get back to her; but I did take up jogging on the beach before work, telling myself it was as much to get fitter as to dissipate anger. But I still woke up in the middle of the night with the familiar hot constriction in my chest. I was well aware that the hold-up was only part of the reason for my anger towards Eddie – the other part was his treatment of Frankie. My mind seemed to take perverse pleasure in picturing her in the most horrific scenes of abuse; and to divert it, I made myself think of the last time we were together in the motel room – just as tortuous, in a different sense.

I resorted to mulling over ways I could accidentally bump into her without Eddie's knowledge. I had no idea if she'd moved back to Sydney (maybe they'd just been visiting when he committed the assault) and even if she had, what were the chances of an encounter amongst three million other residents?

I'd finally drift off just before dawn, to be woken by the alarm two hours later, feeling as if I'd just been through the fast cycle of a washing machine.

After one such night, I bought a coffee on the way to work in an effort to wake myself up. I barely had time to sit down and take a sip when my office phone rang.

'Yes,' I said tersely, before remembering that I was at work and supposed to be nice to people who rang wanting help. 'Nice guy' was how people, especially women, used to describe me. What happened to me?

'Will?'

I sat up straight. Suddenly I didn't need the coffee.

'Frankie! Good to hear from you.'

'I'm sorry for what I said when you rang. I didn't mean it.'

'I imagine you're under a lot of strain. What's he been doing to you, Frankie?'

Miniscule pause. 'Look, I'm okay, really.'

I let that ride. 'Are you living in Sydney now?"

'Yes. In Strathfield.'

'Can we meet up sometime?'

Silence.

'Just for coffee?'

I heard her take a deep breath.

'It's up to you,' I said. 'You name the time and venue.'

She blew out a sigh. 'It will have to be a day when Aimee's in day care.'

'You've got a kid?'

'Two. A boy and a girl, five and three. Jake's in kindy.'

The pride in her voice was unmistakable.

'Congratulations. I'm happy for you, I know how badly you wanted a family.'

'Yeah. Look, I have to go to work now. I can meet you on Friday morning. In the city would be best.'

I checked my calendar. I had a seminar all day Friday on Dealing with Resistant Clients. I'd cancel my attendance. Delia wouldn't be happy, but so be it.

We arranged to meet up at 11o'clock at The Den near Hyde Park. I stared out my office window, at the drab sky and the rain sprinkling over the deserted construction site next door. Letting the notion of Frankie as a mother seep into my mind. I had no doubt she'd heap all the love and attention she'd never had herself on her children. But they were Eddie's children. And they were living in a home in which there was domestic violence. I'd bet my life that the assault conviction was just the tip of the iceberg. I felt an intense pity for two children I'd never even met.

Chapter 21

I was at a corner table in The Den by 10.45. It was trendily minimalistic, with rough-hewn tables, bench seats with chintzy cushions and abstract paintings jostling for prominence on the walls. The clientele were businessmen and hipsters with laptops. My mobile phone beeped with a text message. It was Steph.

'Hi bro. Have you been spirited away by aliens? Hope you're okay, give me a call some time.'

'Sorry, been busy. Will phone you later today,' I messaged back. I slid my phone back in my pocket, looked up and there she was. Everything and nothing had changed. Still the same hair and brash lipstick but she'd toned down the eye make-up. Although she was wearing jeans and a turtleneck jumper, her figure was noticeably more rounded. Still the same perfume, though. Desire flared up instantly in a Pavlovian response.

Frankie pulled up a chair and sat down.

'How are you?' I said.

'I'm okay.'

She smiled. It wasn't her 100 kilowatt smile, but it was a worthy effort. There were lines on her face that hadn't been there before and shadows under her eyes. A faint discolouration underneath her right eye looked like a fading bruise.

Silence. Heavy with words unsaid, because I didn't know how to say them or even what they were. Finally I said, 'Are you working?'

'Just the usual. I'm doing rental bond cleans for Clean as a Whistle. It's pretty full-on, not like cleaning hotel rooms, where you can sneak in a tea break.' She looked bashful. 'They just made me team leader. It's weird, I've never thought of myself in a position where I could tell people what to do.'

That strange mix of feistiness and self-deprecation was one of the things I loved about her.

'Congratulations, I think you'll do pretty well. You've always struck me as being a bossy-boots.'

I smiled as I said it and she returned my smile. Warmth flooded me. I desperately wanted to reach over and take her hand, but thought better of it.

'So what made you decide to come back to Sydney?' I asked.

'Eddie's mum's got leukaemia. They've given her five to seven years, but it could be sooner. So we decided to move back, mainly for the kids' sake. I never knew my grandparents when I was a kid, and I think every kid should have at least one grandparent who spoils them rotten and tells them stories about the good old days.' She gave a weary half-smile. 'That's the theory anyhow.'

The waitress delivered our coffees. Frankie emptied two sachets of sugar into her coffee and stirred it vigorously. 'So let's talk about you. Are you still charging broke people the earth so they don't go bankrupt?'

'Actually, I'm not. I'm on the other end of the spectrum, trying to prevent people becoming bankrupt in the first place.'

I told her about my decision to quit law four years ago and how it had taken me 12 months to find the job I really wanted. 'I really enjoy my work. It can be frustrating sometimes; the people I deal with can drive you up the wall. But for those who are motivated, I can really help them get their finances on track and it's life-changing for them. And it more than makes up for the meagre salary.'

'That's good to hear,' Frankie said. 'You seem more relaxed. I never liked that trust-me-I'm -a -lawyer bullshit.'

'Really? And what else have you deduced about me, Ms Freud?'

'Well, I know you're married. But I don't have to be Freud to work that out.' She nodded at the wedding ring on my left hand.

'Yeah.' That was always going to come up, sooner or later. 'Sarah and I got married a bit over three years ago. We'd been friends for some time – she was the assistant manager of The Three Monkeys.'

'Does she have blonde hair? Sort of chunky?'

'That's her.' I smiled inwardly. Sarah would hate to hear herself described as chunky, even though she was back then.

'When I was up on stage singing with you, I noticed her staring at me. She looked put out. No wonder – she had the hots for you.'

Sarah had never mentioned that night after we started dating, nor asked me anything more about Frankie, which I was relieved about.

'Do you have any kids?' Frankie asked.

I shook my head. 'We've been trying for the past year, but no luck. Anyway, tell me about your kids.'

She dug into her handbag, took out her wallet, slid out a photo and handed it to me. 'That was taken a couple of months ago. Aimee was having a whinge day – it took ages to get her to smile.'

I studied the two chubby-cheeked, clear-eyed children sitting together against a background of muted blue and pink. The boy's blonde hair glinted with red tinges and he had the endearingly cheeky smile of a kid who knew he could get away with anything. The girl had a mop of brown curly hair and her mother's eyes, and although she was smiling, you could imagine her expression changing from sunny to thundery in an instant, at the drop of an ill-timed word. She was a miniature Frankie.

'That's Aimee with a double "e",' Frankie said.

'They're beautiful kids,' I said. And I meant it. Photos of other people's kids left me indifferent, but there was something about Frankie's kids... maybe that was it. They were her kids. I'd love them if they had two heads.

'Jake's full name is Jacob, after my brother,' Frankie said. I studied Jake again. There was some resemblance to Frankie's brother, from what I could remember from his photo, in that he had also been blonde-haired and blue-eyed as a child. But I could see little resemblance to Eddie, although I had only seen his face from a distance in the courtroom. Time distorts memories by overlaying them with other memories and gaps are filled in by the imagination and prejudice. I had no idea whether the image I had of Eddie now was accurate.

'Are you enjoying being back in Sydney?' I asked.

She twirled her coffee cup around in its saucer. 'It hasn't turned out the way I hoped. Maureen, that's Eddie's Mum, is a cranky old bitch; and when we take the kids for a visit, she just ignores them and whinges all the time about the treatment from her doctors. Jake told me the other day he doesn't want to go to Grandma's any more because she scares him. I know she's not well, but I thought she might have made an effort for the kids' sake.'

Her voice wavered. 'I have these pictures in my mind of how life's going to be, and it never works out that way.'

So the cottage with the white picket fence, and Mum and Dad cuddling on the couch hadn't eventuated with Eddie. Surprise, surprise.

'Yeah, reality sucks all right.'

'But I'm glad you're happy anyway,' Frankie said.

'What makes you think that?

She stared at me.

'Sure, I've got a job I enjoy, I didn't even mind giving up the Audi, and a wife who loves me. But happy? Before today, I had some idea in the back of my mind that I could achieve a state of contentment. But now that I've seen you again, that's flown out the window.'

'What do you mean?' Frankie said in a small voice. I took her hand in both of mine. She didn't pull it away.

'Frankie, you're the only woman I want. I've loved you every day of the past six years and I love you now. I can't tell you how much...' I swallowed the lump in my throat and started again. 'We could have a life together – I know you're not happy with Eddie. If you can find the courage to leave him, I'll leave my marriage too and we can start afresh. We can even go interstate if you think we'll be safer. With the kids, of course.'

Frankie's eyes were tearing up. She brushed the tears away fiercely.

'It's not that simple. I've already left him a couple of times, and he found out where I was and threatened to kill me if I didn't come home. And as a father he's got rights. He'd take me to Family Court to apply for access, then I'd have to go to court as well, interstate or not.'

'Why don't you take out a domestic violence order out against him? You'd have excellent grounds because of the assault. In fact, I'm surprised the police didn't take one out anyway.'

I knew the police could apply to the courts for a domestic violence order against a perpetrator, even if the victim didn't want it, and that if they deemed the victim's life in danger they could also request no-contact conditions on the order.

'They did,' Frankie said. 'But by the time it got to court, Eddie had started anger management counselling. So the magistrate just made a standard order to be of good behaviour.'

Meaning Eddie could continue living with Frankie – until the next time, when he killed her. Of course he was going to anger management counselling – he knew how to manipulate the justice system. Counselling would have as much impact on him as Zen Buddhism would have on a terrorist.

'We both know that's not going to change anything,' I said. 'You need to get out now. Before he kills you. Or the kids.'

'He wouldn't hurt the kids,' she said sharply. 'He adores them.'

'He's hurting them by being violent towards you. That has a big impact on them, how they grow up and learn to behave.'

'I fucking know that!'

She dug into her handbag, took out a tissue and swiped again at her tears. 'There's something else. Remember at the hotel, when you asked me what hold Eddie had over me? He's threatened to tell the cops I drove the getaway car for the robbery if I leave him.'

'Wouldn't it be worth facing the music to get him out of your life? You wouldn't necessarily go to jail – he forced you at knifepoint for God's sake – that's got to count for something! I could get you a good lawyer.'

She shook her head. 'I can't take the risk. If I go to jail...' she stifled a sob. 'I couldn't do that to the kids.'

A mobile phone beeped. She reached into her handbag and pulled out her mobile phone.

'Is that him checking up on you?'

She didn't answer, just read the message and put her phone back in her bag.

'Where does he think you are now?'

'He thinks I'm at work. I took a sickie.'

'So you lost a day's pay to see me?'

She nodded, avoiding my gaze. 'I don't know why. There's no point; I can't go away with you. And there's no point in me seeing you again because it only makes it worse.' She pushed her chair back. 'And I have to go."

'Wait, sit down for a minute.'

Frankie perched on the edge of her seat, poised for exit.

'I just want one thing before you go. Tell me you love me.'

'Oh, for fuck's sake!'

'Please?'

'Do you promise to leave me alone if I do?'

'Yes.'

'I fucking love you.'

'Do you mean it?'

'You didn't say I had to mean it.'

'But do you?'

I willed her to look at me and in her eyes I saw what I needed to see.

'Okay, I fucking love you and I fucking mean it. Satisfied?'

I grinned. 'Francis Slater, you are without a doubt the most romantic woman I've ever known.'

I slid around on to her seat and cupped my hands around her face. I pressed my lips on to hers. She resisted at first then softened into the kiss. I drew away and she shivered as I trailed my fingers down her neck. Before she could stop me, I rolled down the collar of her turtleneck jumper. She pulled away. But it was too late. I'd seen the two gigantic yellow-brown bruises circling each side of her neck.

Chapter 22

By the time I was on to my third beer, my warm mellow had deepened to melancholy. After brushing the dust off my guitar, I sat on my deck, serenading the seagulls squawking overhead. I'd hardly touched my guitar over the last few years – the creative part of me had shrivelled up and died, and the sales of my album had dribbled away to nothing, due to lack of promotion. Now a torrent of phrases, riffs and notes spewed out of me – some full of pathos, others explosive with rage, some so tender they were merely a whisper. I should be writing these down, I told myself. But I didn't want to break the spell.

I looked up. Sarah was standing at the sliding door watching me. I hadn't heard her arrive home from work. I looked at my watch. Five-thirty. I had come home straight after my meeting with Frankie with so much going on in my head that I was barely aware of my surroundings.

'Are you all right?' Sarah asked.

'Yeah, just chilling out.'

'How was the seminar?'

'What sem...oh.' I remembered I'd told her about the seminar on resistant clients I was supposed to attend. 'It was okay. Nothing I didn't know already.'

'I haven't seen you play the guitar for ages.'

'I just got the urge. I didn't realise how much I've missed it.'

'I'm glad.' Sarah moved behind me and started massaging the back of my neck. I groaned with pleasure and leaned into it. 'I was so disappointed when you stopped playing – you need to, it's part of you who you are. Not to mention wasting your talent. You should go back to doing hotel gigs, even make another album.'

'Maybe. How was your day, anyway?'

'Pretty intense. Frogmarch are doing a tour and staying at our city hotel on the weekend, so I've been preparing for that. Some of these groups make the most outrageous demands. These guys want fresh chilled mango, truffles and French champagne for breakfast. And silk sheets on the beds. And they're barely out of high school.'

Her voice was weary. She enjoyed her job – she was a born organiser – but the hours were long. It was entirely due to her salary that we'd been able to keep my beachfront apartment. But sometimes I wondered if she resented the responsibility and felt tied down.

'Yeah, they expect it all on a plate as soon as they have their first hit song. Listen to me, disillusioned old muso at the age of thirty-eight.' I gently removed her hands from my neck. 'I should be doing this to you. How about you go and have a long soak in the bath and I'll cook dinner.'

'I'd love that.' She slid her arms around my neck. 'You're so good to me.'

I'm not good to you at all. I'm a lousy husband. I'm in love with another woman, and this morning I was discussing leaving you and running away with her.

#

As I chopped up vegetables for the curry, I replayed the morning's events in my head for the umpteenth time. The bruises on Frankie's neck had loomed in my mind all day. She'd said that the incident had happened a few weeks ago. She didn't go into details and I didn't press her – she was barely holding it together.

'I've started seeing a domestic violence counsellor,' she'd said, as if that was the magic wand that would make everything better.

'That's a very good step but right now you need more than counselling. You need to get right away from Eddie. I was serious when I said he'll kill you. Do you want your kids to grow up without a mother?'

It was a low blow, but I couldn't help it.

'Don't say that,' Frankie whispered. I drew her to me and brushed her tears away. She disentangled herself from me and got up. 'Please don't contact me. He'll find out.'

And she walked out.

I had no intention of keeping my word to her about leaving her alone. How could I? I'd never forgive myself if Eddie killed her. Why hadn't the police and the magistrate seen through Eddie's façade? He must be more persuasive than I gave him credit for – or was Frankie one of those who had fallen through the cracks of an overloaded justice system? Somehow I had to persuade her to pack herself and the kids up, and escape with me.

Chapter 23

I sat bolt upright in bed. The bedside clock said it was 2.20 am. I was instantly awake, my mind buzzing. Over the last three days since I'd seen Frankie, something about her son Jake had been needling me. Something was not right. Now it was falling into place.

I slipped out of bed, careful not to wake Sarah. I pulled on a pair of boxer shorts and padded out to the living room. I poured myself a drink of water and sat on the living room couch in the darkness. I mulled over the facts. Frankie and I had made love two weeks before Eddie was released. Six years ago. Jake looked nothing like Frankie or Eddie. I wouldn't mind betting he'd arrived early – two weeks, in fact.

I went into the study, switched on the light and rifled around on one of the shelves until I found an album of photos my mother had given me as soon as Sarah and I got back from our honeymoon.

'You might want to show your own children photos of yourself when you were a child,' she'd said. Subtle as a brick.

I flipped through the pages to my first day at school. There I was, swimming in my oversized school shirt and baggy shorts, clutching my Donald Duck backpack. Squarish shaped head, ginger-glinted blonde hair and solemn brown eyes denoting the importance of the occasion. An unmistakable likeness to the photo of Jake that Frankie had shown me. It confirmed what I already suspected. He was my son.

#

The view from our café was worth the early morning rise. Through the trees, the Harbour Bridge curved gracefully into the sapphire-blue sky like a giant dolphin. The harbour, flecked with white sails, shimmered in the sun; if you looked at it long enough, it mesmerised you. Spring was giving us a taste of the long hot summer to come. Sarah had scheduled a breakfast meeting with a client; and when he cancelled at the last minute, she suggested I come instead.

I finished my Eggs Benedict and sat back, replete. Sarah smiled.

'You seem happier lately.'

'Do I?'

'You don't jump down my throat any more when I say something you disagree with. I've noticed the change since you took up your music again. It's a good outlet for you.'

She was right. I hadn't thought about it in that context, but it was true I always felt a sense of release after a session on the guitar. I had almost created enough new songs to make another album – if I wanted to.

'Have you thought about doing any more sessions with Maria?'

Maria had phoned again and left messages about booking another appointment, but she'd given up when I hadn't returned her calls.

'I've been very busy at work lately; it's hard to get time off.'

Sarah gave me a knowing smile. 'That's man-talk for "I'm avoiding the issue because I don't want to go back."'

I swallowed my irritation and refrained from replying. A mobile phone started ringing and I realised it was coming from the pocket of my trousers.

'Aren't you going to answer it?' Sarah said.

'It won't be anything important. They can leave a message.'

I didn't answer it because I knew with a deep certainty it was Frankie. I'd rung the head office of 'Clean as a Whistle' (after racking my brains to remember the company's name) the day before and left a message for her to ring me urgently. It was the only way I could get in touch with her without Eddie knowing. It was just my luck she'd ring when I couldn't take the call. If she was at head office now, I might catch her if I rang back straight away.

Sarah looked at her watch. 'I've got time for another quick coffee. Do you want one?'

I shook my head. 'You order one, I'm going to the Men's.'

I went into one of the cubicles and took out my phone. There were no messages, so I checked the missed calls. There was one from an unknown mobile number. I rang it and a woman's voice answered. 'This is Ellen.'

'This is Will McPherson. I just received a missed call from this number.'

'I'm a friend of Frankie's. I'll hand you over.'

'What's so urgent?' Frankie demanded.

'Is Jake my son?'

Now that I'd said the words out loud, they rang with the air of truth. The silence that followed confirmed it.

'Yes.' Her tone was low.

'You know that for sure?'

'I haven't had him tested, of course. Eddie thinks Jake is his; he's got no reason not to think that. But he was early arriving and...' she faltered, 'he is so like you.'

'Why didn't you tell me the other day?'

'I was going to...but in the end I couldn't. What good would it have done?'

'A lot of good. This changes everything, Frankie. I'm Jake's father and I'm responsible for his well-being.'

'Try telling that to Eddie.'

The door of the Men's squeaked open. 'I can't talk now. Where are you working today?'

'Burwood.'

'Give me the address, and I'll come and see you in your lunch break.'

'We don't get a lunch break. We've got to finish this house today.'

'I'll come and talk to you while you're cleaning. Just for a few minutes.'

'If you're going to try and persuade me to run away with you, don't bother.'

'I'm won't,' I lied.

She gave me the address and I rang off, exiting the cubicle to the curious stare of the man standing at the urinal, who had undoubtedly overheard me arranging my clandestine meeting.

When I got back to our table, Sarah was drinking her second coffee. 'Everything all right?' she asked.

'Yeah, fine.'

Chapter 24

I had a full morning of clients and a lunchtime presentation on our services at the local neighbourhood centre, so it was three o'clock before I turned up at the house in Burwood. I breathed a sigh of relief when I spied a station wagon emblazoned with 'Clean as a Whistle' parked in the street. The house was a double-storey brick with elaborate carved columns over the front porch. The front door was wide open, so I walked in.

'Hullo!' My voiced echoed – the house was cavernous without furniture. A vacuum cleaner hummed from somewhere on the top floor.

A woman appeared from a room up the hallway. Large and homely, hair tied back with a scarf and a cloth in her hand.

'Hi, I'm Will. Are you Ellen?'

'Sure am. Frankie told me you'd be dropping by.'

'Great. Is she upstairs?'

'Yeah, but before you go up...' She approached me, chewing gum as if her life depended on it. 'Frankie's told me about you,' she said in a low voice. 'That you want her to go away with you. I tell her "Go!" but she's too scared. Too scared to go and too scared to stay. That scum of the earth...'

She stopped chewing for a fraction of a second. 'He's been on ice since they came back to Sydney. Not a week doesn't go by when he doesn't get stuck into her. One time she came to work with cigarette burns on her hand. She took the kids and came to my place one night, and somehow he found out where she'd gone and literally dragged her back. He told us both that if we called the police we'd be dead meat. He threatened me!' She beat her ample chest in emphasis. 'I was ropable! She reckons he's got a gun...'

The hum of the vacuum cleaner had stopped, and Frankie was coming down the stairs. Her hair was limp, her face flushed and her apron was adorned with grease stains. She looked stunning.

'I thought you were coming at lunchtime,' she said.

'You said you didn't have a lunch break,' I reminded her. 'And I couldn't get away before now.'

'Go and have a break,' Ellen said. 'I'll finish upstairs.'

'And no having it off on the nice, clean carpet!' she called over her shoulder.

Frankie grinned. 'You're forgetting who's boss round here!'

She led me out through the living room to a small enclosed patio. We perched on the edge of the doorway.

'What do you want to talk about?' she asked. 'As if I didn't know.'

'I'm still coming to grips with it. Being a father, I mean. Sarah and I have been trying for over a year to have a baby. She's talking about going to doctors and getting tested. I thought I might have a low sperm count or something ... but obviously not.'

She took my hand and squeezed it. It was the first time she'd initiated any physical contact between us. 'I really wish he wasn't yours. It just complicates things. Things could have been so different...'

Her eyes welled up. I put my arms around her and buried my face in her hair. It smelled of apples and summer.

'It still can be different. I know you think it's too late, but it's not. Ellen had a word with me before you came down about what he's been doing to you. Don't be upset with her – she's concerned about you.'

'I'm not upset with her. I've only known her since I started this job, but she's been a good friend. My only friend – Eddie's scared the others away.'

She dug into her apron pocket, pulled out a tissue and blew her nose. 'She's always telling me to leave him. And I've tried. I took the kids and went to a shelter a few months ago, but he sent me a text message threatening to track me down and kill me as soon as I left. And I can't report his threats to the police because he says he'll tell them about me driving the getaway car. The only reason he was charged with this,' – she indicated her neck – 'was because we were in the garage, and he was yelling at me and the neighbours called the police.' She twisted her hands. 'He's got a gun.'

'Has he threatened you with it?'

'Not outright, but he showed it to me one day. Just casually, in the course of conversation, all very friendly. But the meaning was clear – if I don't do what he wants, he'll use it. As soon as he went out I turned the house upside down looking for it, but I couldn't find it.'

She gave a half-sigh, half-sob. 'I really thought we were going to make it. He was good for the first couple of years after prison – he had a job in construction, he was off the drugs, we had Jake and then I got pregnant with Aimee. We were happy, as happy as I thought I would ever be. Then he started a new job working away from home. Those guys were into ice so he got back into it, but he was clever enough not to get caught out while he was on parole. It's been heaps worse since we moved back to Sydney. You know what I wished the other day?'

'What?'

'I wished he'd do another hold-up so he'd go to jail and get out of my life. That's terrible, isn't it? To wish that on some other poor victims.'

I stroked her hair. 'Not at all, it's perfectly understandable. I wish you'd told me all this before, instead of trying to cope with it all yourself.'

'I couldn't, you of all people. I brought myself up despite my crap foster carers and being sexually abused, and I've made my own way in the world without help from anyone. No way was I going to admit that I was frightened of Eddie. I feel ashamed of having to give in to him all the time to save myself from being beaten up. The counsellors say, "you shouldn't be ashamed, it's not your fault" but I do feel ashamed, so stop fucking telling me how I should feel!'

'Hold on – what do you mean, you couldn't tell me, of all people?'

Frankie looked away at a couple of sparrows squabbling in a tree at the fence. 'I didn't want you to think I was a loser.'

'Jesus, Frankie, how could you think that? I love you, you can tell me anything and I'd never call you a loser. Or even think it. You are the most beautiful, bravest woman I know.'

'Don't say that.' Her voice trembled. 'You'll make me cry again and I have to get back to work.'

'All right, let's make this quick. I know I said I wasn't going to try and persuade you to go away with me, but I lied. Lawyer's prerogative.'

'Okay, let's do it.'

I'd braced myself for more resistance. 'Really?'

She drew a deep breath. 'Yesterday morning, Eddie went out really early and Jake came into my bed with me and said, "Mummy, when is Daddy coming home?" And I said I didn't know and he said, "I don't want him to come home, I get scared when he yells. I like it when there's just you and me, and Aimee. " '

My heart twisted in my chest at the thought of Jake, my son, being frightened of the one person who was supposed to take care of him and protect him. That was me now.

'I've been thinking about it since you rang this morning. I have to find the courage to go. For the kids. I can do it if you're with me.'

I held her close to me, and her body relaxed into mine. For a few perfect moments, we sat in the cooling afternoon air and for the first time I dared to think about a life with Frankie.

Frankie drew away. 'What about your wife?'

'I'll tell her tonight.'

I didn't even want to think about that.

'Are you sure you're doing the right thing for yourself? You're breaking up a marriage for me.'

'If I'd ever thought there was a chance you and I could be together, I'd never have married Sarah. And to be perfectly honest, I married her because she was around; we'd known each other for years and I knew she loved me. Like you, I thought I'd be the happiest it was possible to be. And it's been fine; she's a good person. It's going to be horrible telling her. But I have you now and I have a son – we have a son.'

'Haven't you two finished yet?' Ellen's voice floated out from inside.

We both jumped up and I gave Frankie a long, hard kiss. 'Think of a plan of escape – the best way we can do it as soon as possible. Can I ring you tomorrow on Ellen's phone?'

Frankie nodded. 'Good luck with Sarah.' She hesitated. 'I feel bad for her.'

Chapter 25

'What do you mean there's someone else?'

Sarah had turned deathly pale. I couldn't bear to look at her.

'Her name's Frankie. I met her a few years ago, before you and I got together. And she's come back into my life again.'

'Frankie – isn't that the woman you got up on stage to sing with you that time?'

'Yes.'

'I thought at the time there was something between the two of you. So when did this Frankie' – she spat out the name – 'come back into your life?'

'A few weeks ago.'

We were sitting on the living room couch after dinner. Sarah had the TV remote control in her hand, about to press the 'on' button, when I broke the news to her. I thought she was going to throw it at me, but instead she threw it on the coffee table and put her hands over her face. 'God, I don't believe it! Tell me it's not true.'

After a few moments of agonising silence, she took her hands away from her face and looked me in the eye. 'And of course you've been screwing her.'

'Actually I haven't.' Technically it was true. She hadn't asked about hugging or kissing.

'You really expect me to believe that?'

'It's true. She's in a relationship with a violent partner.' I owed her the truth so I told her everything, starting from when I first met Frankie in court, while Sarah stared at me, wild-eyed.

'I can't believe she's the girlfriend of the guy who held you up! You're planning to run off with a woman who screws an armed robber and God knows who else?'

I said nothing. I wasn't in a position to protest about her slur on Frankie's sexual behaviour.

'And I suppose she's got a tribe of kids?'

'Two.' I took a deep breath. 'I'm sorry, there's no easy way to break this to you. One of them is mine. He's five, he was conceived just before Gisbourne got out of jail.'

'God, it just gets worse.' She put her hands over her face again and her shoulders shook as she sobbed silently. I stared at the blank TV screen, desperately wanting to reach out and comfort her. She looked up, red-eyed. "I hope you're happy; you've got the child you wanted.'

'I'm sorry. I know it's horrible for you to hear that. It was a shock to me too – I didn't find out till very recently. Which is one of the reasons I have to go. I have a responsibility to him now to raise him as best I can. Frankie and I are taking the children and probably heading off interstate.'

'Very noble of you – all for your son's sake, of course. Not because you want to run off and bang some chick who's been hanging out with the scum of the earth all her life.'

She shook her head. 'I just don't get this.' She looked at me as if I were an insect under a microscope. 'And I don't get you, Will. Suddenly I have no idea who the hell you are. I've been married to a complete stranger for the past three years.'

She picked up her car keys from the kitchen sideboard. 'I'm going out. And you'd better be gone by the time I get back.'

Chapter 26

I threw some clothes and toiletries into an overnight bag and booked into a motel down the road. I could have stayed with my parents, but I wasn't in the mood for explanations right now. Or disapproval. Most of my friends, also lawyers, had drifted away after I left the profession; and the couple I was still in contact with had wives and families, and I didn't want to impose on them.

I watched TV until midnight, with no recollection of what I'd seen, and went to bed. But thoughts and memories whirling around in my head kept me wide awake. Sarah and me, the first time we made love at her place, when she'd blurted out that she loved me as she made me scrambled eggs the next morning, our garden wedding on a sparkling spring day, the sun shining on our marriage, my parents smiling and clapping, happy that I'd married a girl they liked and approved of. The expression on Sarah's face when I broke the news, how swift and terrible was the anger and hurt and the ultimatum to leave. Not that I blamed her for one moment. She'd done absolutely nothing wrong except love me. I was now one of those men I'd always despised, who left their wife for another woman.

When I eventually drifted off to sleep, I had a nightmare in which Eddie was chasing me down a dark alley brandishing a knife; and when he caught me, he morphed into Sarah. She was just about to plunge the knife into me when I woke up. It was 10 o'clock and the sun was streaming in through the curtains. I'd forgotten to set my phone alarm. I sprang out of bed and checked my phone. Two missed calls from Delia. I rang her back and said I'd be there in half an hour.

#

I apologised profusely to Delia. She regarded me with concern. 'You haven't been yourself lately. Is everything all right at home?'

'Yes, fine.' I suddenly realised I'd have to give notice. I'd do it tomorrow; I couldn't face it today.

I tried to keep my mind on the task at hand as I saw my first client of the day, a young man with dreadlocks and dull eyes, who didn't want to hear the news that he'd have to give up smoking weed to pay off his phone and credit card debts. As soon as he was out the door, I phoned Ellen. She answered and handed me over to Frankie.

'How did you go last night?' she asked.

'Not good. She threw me out, so I'm staying at a motel down the road.'

'I'm so sorry. I feel terrible, Will. You're breaking up your marriage for me but I want you to; so I feel bad about that and if I try not to feel bad about it, I feel bad about not feeling bad, and I want to start a new life with you more than anything, you, me and the kids but I'm really scared...'

'Listen, Frankie, I know you're feeling bad about my marriage. We're both feeling bad, but your life takes precedence. Your life, just as much as our life. Have you thought about a plan of escape?'

'Yes. I don't think you should come to the house, Eddie's too unpredictable. He's lost his job and sometimes he's away all day, and other times he mopes around the house, looking for things to go psycho about. I think it should just happen on a normal work day, and I'll do the normal routine things. I'll get ready for work, and get Jake and Aimee ready for kindy and day care. I'll leave the house at the usual time, and then I'll meet you somewhere, and we can swap cars and go.'

'Where should we meet?'

'There's a park down the road from the day care; we can meet there.'

'And you'll just leave your car there?'

'Unless you've got a better suggestion.'

'I don't like that idea. An abandoned car will get the police involved. They'll trace the registration and when they find out you and the kids have disappeared, they might start thinking along the lines of abduction and murder. Next thing you know, there's a police alert out for you and our cover's blown. I suppose you can't catch a bus or train?'

'If Eddie's home, he'll ask me why I'm not taking the car. He'll be suspicious straight away.'

I thought for a few moments. 'There's no way around it. I'll have to come and pick you up from the house. It will have to be a spur-of-the-moment thing – you pick a time after Eddie's left the house and you know he's going to be away for a while, text me straight away and I'll come and get you.'

'I still don't like the idea of you coming to the house. What if I wait until Eddie goes out, then the kids and I will walk to the shops. There's a little shopping centre a couple of blocks away called The Groves – you can meet us there.'

'Okay. Where would you like to go?'

'What about Gosford? I think it would be kind of nice to live in the same town where Jake lived. And Colin and Leonie are only an hour's drive away.'

'That's a great idea. Maybe we can book into the same motel we stayed in, for old time's sake.'

'You're such a romantic.' I could hear the smile in her voice. 'But what if Eddie puts out a missing persons report on me?'

'When we get to Gosford, we'll go to the police, tell them the story and that we don't want your whereabouts divulged for safety reasons. They can pass on the message that you're alive and well if Eddie starts kicking up a fuss.'

'You've got more trust in the cops than I have. But I guess we don't have a choice.'

'We need to do this as soon as we can. From now on, I'll have my phone on me 24/7 and as soon as the opportunity comes up, text me. Use your own phone this time. Eddie won't have a chance to get hold of it. Wait for my reply to make sure I received your message, grab the kids and go straight to the shopping centre. Don't pack anything – that'll slow you down – just leave with what you're wearing. We can buy new stuff when we get to Gosford.'

'I never knock back an opportunity to buy new gear.' She paused. 'Have you told your family?"

'Not yet, I'll tell them today.'

'I know what they'll say – what are you doing, throwing away a good job and marriage to go off with some crim's used and abused girlfriend from the wrong side of the tracks?'

She was spot on there; only they wouldn't put it quite so crudely.

'I'm a big boy, I can handle it. I've got to go; I've got a client waiting. Be brave, baby, and it will all work out, you'll see. And remember I love you.'

'Ditto.' The smile was there again in her voice.

Chapter 27

My parents' reaction was as I'd expected. As I sat in their living room, with Steph present as well, all eyes were on me as I briefly recounted the facts in an objective, lawyerly fashion. I wished I'd taken the coward's way out and phoned them. But I knew I'd be glad later that I hadn't.

Shock, horror and, of course, disapproval. But muted, as if I'd exhausted those emotions in them and this was what they expected of me now. My father just shook his head and said 'Jesus Christ' several times instead of his usual ranting. My mother was the vocal one, with the predictable comments about being selfish, throwing my life away and how could I do this to Sarah? But they were uttered with an air of resignation, as if realising they would have no effect on my behaviour. And it was true, their reactions failed to touch me. It was as if I'd grown a hide so thick that no criticism or condemnation could penetrate it.

The phone rang. My father left the room to answer it, leaving an uncomfortable silence. Steph, who'd been silent up until now, said, 'I always knew you didn't love Sarah. And I figured that when the day came that you fell head over heels with someone else, there'd be problems.'

'Really, dear?' Mum said. 'I had no inkling of that. I thought Will and Sarah made a lovely couple.'

'We did,' I agreed. 'And Steph's right. I don't love Sarah, not in the way I love Frankie. And I admit I made a mistake in marrying her; I've completely stuffed up her life.'

'And this boy, are you sure he's yours?' Mum asked.

'Yes, I'm sure,' I snapped, forestalling any further discussion on the issue.

Mum sighed. 'You have to realise this is a lot for us to take in – I've got another grandson I've never met. Are you going to tell Nick?'

'I'll phone him when I get home.' Thankfully, Nick was at an international law conference in London, so I didn't have to endure him face to face.

Steph came down to the car with me as I was leaving. She refused my help, labouring her way down the front steps, holding on to the railing. When she reached the bottom, I wrapped her in a bear hug. 'I'm so proud of you. The doctors said you'd never get out of your wheelchair, and look at you! You'll be running a triathlon before you know it. I wish I had half your courage.'

'Careful, you'll knock me off my feet and ruin all my efforts,' she laughed. Her face became serious. 'You've got a ton of courage, bro. It took real guts to walk away from your job, and all the income and status that goes with it to be a financial counsellor. And put up with all the family's flak. And it's taking a hell of a lot of guts to do what you're doing now, especially with that Eddie character in the mix. I just hope it's the right decision. For you.'

'Don't worry, it's the right decision. For me, Frankie and the children.'

'Text me as soon as you get to Gosford. Then I can breathe a sigh of relief. And don't worry about Nick – block your ears. Or even better, hang up on him.'

#

It was 10 pm by the time I got back to my motel. I'd moved to one in Lidcombe, closer to Frankie, so that I could be at The Groves shopping centre within 15 minutes of her calling. I rang Nick, but his phone went straight to voicemail so I left a message. He rang back just as I was getting into bed.

'I've already heard the news,' he said. So Mum had been in his ear already – or maybe it was Steph, warning him to soften the impact on me.

'I don't know what the hell you think you're doing. Throwing your life down the toilet to go on the run with this tart and her kids. Do you realise Gisbourne will kill you if he finds you?'

'Let me deal with that,' I said. 'And we're not going on the run; we're going interstate to start a new life.'

Why did I bother explaining? He never listened.

Nick was talking to someone in the background. 'What? Look, sorry, I've got to go. I'm giving a presentation in a few minutes. For God's sake, be careful. I don't want to see you in the headlines of next Sunday's tabloids.'

I was just about to say, 'I'll try not to spoil your breakfast,' but I stopped myself. For once, I resisted getting sucked into the usual verbal slanging match. I mustered a tone of warmth and sincerity. 'Thanks for your concern, I appreciate it.'

There was a pause. 'No worries. Keep in touch,' Nick muttered.

That was the first time in my living memory he'd said those words.

#

I gave notice to Delia as soon as I arrived at work. Despite her curious but gentle probing, I hadn't divulged much of my personal life, so I gave her the bare bones. I didn't tell her about the domestic violence or Eddie's threats. I knew she'd be full of motherly concern as it was, without giving her more to worry about. She listened without judgment or comment.

'I'm sorry, I know this is really inconvenient for you. I'm giving two weeks' notice from today. But I'll probably leave sooner.'

Delia sighed. 'It certainly is inconvenient. It's very difficult to find people with financial expertise and counselling skills. But I'm just as concerned about you. That's a big step you're taking, I just hope it works out for you.' She patted my arm. 'I'll miss you. And so will the clients. Remember Noah, the young chap who got cranky when you told him he'd have to give up cannabis?'

I nodded. Noah had stalked out in a sulk, refusing to make another appointment.

'He rang yesterday after you'd left for the day and asked me to pass on a message. He said he'd cut his weed down from $100 to $50 a week. And he's going to pay off his drug debts then come in and see you.'

I grinned. 'It's a step forward – cutting down the cannabis anyway. Not so sure about the drug debts. But I'm sure you'll be able to handle his cheek.'

Chapter 28

It had been a week since I'd left home. I'd sent a couple of text messages to Sarah asking how she was, but she'd replied with 'Go away and leave me alone'. I decided to try phoning this time; so after a dinner of tough steak and overcooked vegetables in the motel restaurant, I rang her.

To my surprise, she answered. 'What do you want?'

'I just wanted to see if you're okay.'

'As if you'd care. Have you left yet?'

'No. Can we meet up some time soon? I don't want to go without seeing you and well ... explaining things.'

'I don't want to hear your pathetic explanations. I always knew you didn't love me in the same way I loved you; but I thought it didn't matter, that it would change over the years and we could still have a good life together. Pretty naïve, wasn't I?'

'No, you weren't. It could easily have happened if...'

'Yeah, the big if. And in answer to your question, no, I don't want to meet up, just so you can try to salve your conscience with your excuses and justifications.'

'There won't be any excuses or justifications. I just want to tell you how it is. And that it's nothing to do with anything that you've said or done or not said or done. You've been great, more than I deserve.'

She gave a bitter laugh. 'The old "it's not you, it's me" line.'

'Please, Sarah, just give me this one chance to talk to you.'

She gave a sigh of exasperation. 'Okay, tomorrow afternoon at 2 pm. Not at home. Hannah's Cafe around the corner.'

Tomorrow was Saturday. I had nothing planned except sitting around waiting for Frankie's text message.

'Thanks, I really appreciate it. See you then.'

Chapter 29

I sat in my motel room trying to concentrate on an old Robert Ludlum paperback I'd picked up at the second-hand bookshop down the road. I'd been restless all week since speaking to Frankie, feeling trapped within the four walls of my motel room. But when I went out for a walk in the fresh air, I was too much on edge to enjoy it and ended up coming straight back.

My phone beeped. My heart jumped as I grabbed it. One text message. 'He just left to go fishing, am about to leave. Will be outside Delish Donuts at The Groves in half an hour.'

It was just after 11 o'clock. 'On my way,' I messaged back. I threw my stuff into my bag, went to the motel reception and checked out. Even though I'd already memorised the quickest route from my motel to The Groves shopping centre, I set my car GPS for extra insurance. I estimated I should get there at about the same time as Frankie if there were no traffic hold-ups. As I sat at a red light drumming my fingers on the steering wheel, I suddenly remembered my meeting with Sarah at 2 o' clock. Damn! I couldn't stop now to text her. I'd do it later – if I had time.

The traffic light gods were on my side but I resisted the temptation to speed – the last thing I needed now was to be pulled over for a speeding ticket. I'd taken 15 minutes to pack and check out of my motel, and I arrived at the shopping centre in exactly 15 minutes. Half an hour on the dot. I slotted into a car park outside the bottle shop and got out.

Delish Donuts was diagonally opposite, immediately recognisable with its neon pink, dot-covered doorway, resembling donut icing sprinkled with hundreds and thousands. Frankie stood outside it with Jake and Aimee, one child on each side. They wore backpacks; and as I grew closer, I could see that Aimee was sucking the ear of a soft toy rabbit, and Jake wore a Thomas the Tank Engine cap and was clutching a Lego car. He watched my approach with the intense curiosity that only a five-year-old could muster, and my heart constricted.

'Hi!' I greeted Frankie. The look on her face told me instantly something was wrong. Before I could think, a man with unkempt hair and a dark shadow of stubble stepped out of Delish Donuts holding a paper bag in one hand. The other was in his coat pocket. In the split second I took to register it was Eddie, I grabbed Frankie's hand. 'Let's go.'

Then Eddie was behind me and something jabbed me in the back. 'Not so fast, lover boy,' he said in my ear. He smelled of stale sweat and cigarette smoke. 'You wouldn't want me to use this gun now, would you? Get back in the car – you're gonna take us all for a ride.'

In a panic, I looked around me – surely someone would see what was going on. An old couple were getting into their car nearby and a group of teenage girls chatted noisily outside the pharmacy. No-one was taking any notice.

Eddie jabbed the gun harder into my back. 'No-one's going to help you. Open your mouth and you're dead. Now walk. I'm right on your arse.'

Eddie took Frankie by the arm and pushed her in front of me. 'Same goes for you, bitch. Kids, walk with Mummy.'

'Where are we going, Daddy?' Jake asked.

'For a drive. Shut up and be a good boy, and you can have a doughnut.'

We walked back to my car, Frankie and the kids in front of me.

Jake looked up at Frankie. 'Mummy, why has Daddy got a gun?'

Eddie leapt forward and clipped him hard on the side of the head. 'Shut up! Do you want a doughnut or not?'

Jake gave a loud sob then obviously thinking better of it, toned it down to a snivel. Aimee let out a wail. In my peripheral vision, I saw a couple of heads turn; but a wailing child in a shopping centre was nothing out of the ordinary, and I guessed Eddie had put the gun out of sight.

Frankie leaned down and gave Aimee a hug. 'It's okay, honey.' She made a good job of sounding reassuring.

I unlocked the car and got into the driver's side. Eddie got in beside me. Frankie and the kids, still snivelling, scrambled into the back seat. Frankie helped them to put on their seatbelts.

'Jeez, just a crummy Mazda, I was expectin' at least a Jag,' Eddie said. 'Maybe you're not such a hotshot lawyer after all.' He dug the gun into my ribs. 'Drive. Go out the exit and turn left. And keep your hands on the wheel.'

I did as I was instructed.

'Where are we going, Mummy?' Jake asked in a small voice.

'What did I tell you before?' Eddie yelled. He tossed the paper bag over his shoulder into the back seat. 'Stuff these in your gob and shut up!'

I heard the bag rustle and then silence. I followed Eddie's instructions and we were soon on the motorway heading northwest. I tried to still my racing mind and think rationally. Where was he taking us? Was he going to hold us all hostage somewhere? Or – I could hardly bear to think it – kill us? And how the hell had he discovered Frankie's escape plan? I longed to catch her eye in the rear view mirror, but Eddie was watching my every move.

'Left here,' he commanded as I pulled up at a red light. We were out in a new suburban development that was still half bushland, and the road to the left wound its way through scrub and thickets of trees festooned with lantana, its sweetish smell infiltrating the car. The road became a narrow track and the forest crowded in against the car. Sweat trickled down my neck. *This is not happening – I'm having a nightmare. Soon I will wake up. Please.*

'Where are you taking us?' Frankie asked. She didn't quite succeed in hiding the tremor in her voice.

Eddie spun around and trained the gun on her. 'Shut up, bitch! You disgust me – you and your shit-don't-stink pretty boy. He won't be so pretty when I've finished with him!'

Jake began to sob again. 'Daddy, don't shoot us!' Then Aimee started howling.

'Shhh, both of you, Daddy's not going to shoot you,' Frankie whispered.

Eddie turned around to the front and dug the gun again into my ribs. 'Pull up here.'

We had come to a grassy clearing, which sloped into a small creek, meandering through the trees. I pulled up and turned off the engine. Eddie turned around to Frankie again, the gun aimed at her.

'You stay here. One move and you're dead meat, and I'll bury you with lover boy. Kids, stay here with your mother.' He nudged me with the gun. 'Out.'

So he was going to shoot me. A one-man firing squad with Frankie and the kids as witnesses. Desperation kick-started my brain and in a split second, I had a plan. Of sorts. I was pretty sure Eddie was under the influence of drugs, probably ice. Meaning he'd slip up somehow. It could be our only chance.

Chapter 30

Eddie sprang out of the car and came round to the driver's side, the gun trained on me as I opened the door.

'Over there.'

He nodded in the direction of the creek. I got out of the car, leaving the keys in the ignition. I closed the car door and willed my trembling legs to move. Eddie followed close behind me. He didn't appear to have noticed that I had left the keys in the ignition. Or if he had, he didn't regard it of any consequence. I darted a glance at Frankie through the front windscreen. Her eyes met mine, her expression not changing one iota. But I knew she knew what to do.

It was eerily quiet. Just the leaves rustling in the wind and the faint burble of the creek. The beating in my chest soared above them all, filling my ears.

'Any particular spot?' I asked Eddie over my shoulder. I was playing for time – to give Frankie time.

'Stop where you are.'

I turned around and looked straight at him. The roar of a car engine filled the stillness. My car bounded forward and headed straight for Eddie, Frankie at the wheel. Thank God for automatics with gutsy take-off. Eddie wheeled around. I turned and ran, pounding along the narrow track that led into the bush. I only had a few seconds' grace to get ahead.

A loud crack echoed through the air. A gunshot. I stumbled momentarily with the shock. Had he shot me? I didn't feel anything. *Please God, no! Don't let it be Frankie*! But I knew it was too late for prayers.

'You fucking bastard!' Eddie screamed. I veered off the track into the bush to give me more cover, jumping over vines, pushing through scrub and weaving around bushes. Eddie was crashing his way through the bush behind me. Another gunshot rang out –– the bullet grazed the trunk of a tree several metres away from me. Eddie was losing it. Great. He might have the advantage of ice-fuelled adrenalin and a gun, but I was driven by a powerful anger more intoxicating than any drug – I was Superman, I was invincible. Eddie had shot the woman I loved. Nothing he did could hurt me now. Not even killing me.

My legs and lungs were burning but I kept going, then as suddenly as it had begun, the bushland stopped. The bush track became a gravel road. A sign pointed straight ahead. 'Narrow Springs Estate. Blocks still available.' I was right out in the open, nowhere to hide. I dashed back and ducked behind a large paperbark tree, squeezing myself into the hollow just as Eddie came racing up, panting heavily.

'Jesus fucking Christ,' he grunted.

I edged out of the hollow, around the back of the tree and grabbed him from behind. One arm around his neck, pressing against it with all my strength, the other gripping the arm that held the gun and forcing it down. A shot rang out. Pain exploded in my foot. Eddie wrenched my arm away from his neck; and as he swung around, I drove my fist into his stomach. He grunted and hunched over. I kicked the hand that held the gun, then swiped it out of his grip and threw it as hard as I could into the bush behind me. This wasn't about who had the upper hand with the gun – this was personal. Just Eddie and me.

He went to go after the gun, but I blocked his path and drove my fist into his jaw. It gave a satisfying smack; and as he reeled back, I sprang at him and we both fell to the ground. We rolled around in a tangle of dirt and grass, and grunts and punches. My mouth was full of blood, I was gasping for breath and somewhere in the back of my consciousness I was aware of the pain in my foot. Every time I felt my strength fading, I thought of my beautiful Frankie, her jaw determined as she gripped the steering wheel of my car; and I drove my fist once again into Eddie's flesh.

But Eddie's superior weight and strength gave him the upper hand. Each time I tried to get up, he wrestled me down. He pinned me down and drove his fist into my face. His body felt like a ton of bricks and I couldn't move. He punched me again. This was it – he was going to beat me until I was dead.

My eyes were filled with sweat and dirt, and Eddie's face was just a blur above me. I scrabbled frantically around on the ground with my hands for something I could use as a weapon. My fingers closed around a stick. It felt sturdy. I picked it up and jabbed it hard into Eddie's side.

'Fuck!' he yelled. I jabbed him again, trying to find his rib and on the third jab I felt bone. Eddie groaned and his weight slackened enough for me to roll to one side and scramble out from under him. I limped in the direction of the bush. What in hell was I thinking to throw the gun away? I had to find it before Eddie did.

'You fucking bastard!' Eddie was coming up behind me, his breathing laboured. I bent down, picked up a rock, swung around and threw it. It grazed his shoulder then landed in the grass behind him. He sneered.

'Is that the best you can do, pretty boy?'

His eyes were darting around, obviously looking for the gun. He took off in the direction of a clump of bushes. I looked around, spotted the rock I'd thrown at him and limped towards it. I gritted my teeth through the pain in my foot and ramped up my pace. Eddie bent over and picked something up from the ground. He whipped around and aimed the gun at me.

The rock was in my hand. I threw it, hard and overarm, like a cricket ball. It hit Eddie on the side of the head. At that moment he fired a shot, but it whizzed by me before he crumpled to the ground. I hurried over, picked up the gun from the ground where he'd dropped it and looked down at him.

For a split second I thought I'd killed him; then I noticed his chest moving. I could hardly believe I'd knocked him out – rugby was more my forte than cricket, but then my life had never depended on my bowling prowess. Eddie's face was a bloody mess and his nose was skewed to one side. I probably looked just as bad – I certainly felt it. I dug my mobile phone out of my jeans pocket. The glass had shattered and nothing was working. Damn.

I leaned over and dug into Eddie's jeans pocket, keeping a wary eye on him in case he suddenly came to life. I hauled out a mobile phone. It was then that I noticed that his filthy, grass-streaked clothes were also spattered with blood. Did I do that much damage? I looked down and realised it was coming from me. From my foot, where Eddie had shot me. It was still pouring blood. And hurting like nothing had ever hurt before.

My head was spinning. *Don't pass out now.* The screen on Eddie's phone was miraculously still intact. I turned it on and unlocked the screen. Eddie's eyes fluttered open. He made a movement as if to try and get up. I pointed the gun at his chest. I could shoot him now, rid the world of one vermin and make sure he never hurt another person, woman or man. I had never used a gun in my life, but I had no compunction in making this the first time.

His swollen lip turned up in a sneer. 'Go on, shoot me.'

My hand shook. Eddie's gaze was fixed on me, taunting me. I was limp, my rage draining out of me. Now that I had the opportunity to exact revenge, I had no desire to do it. Killing him was too easy. He didn't deserve a quick death. He deserved to rot in jail for the rest of his life.

I dialled 000 and waited for the police to arrive.

Chapter 31

Maria ushered me into her office. 'This is a pleasant surprise. I didn't think you were coming back.'

I limped over to the armchair in front of her desk. My foot had suffered a lot of tissue damage and it was a long healing process. I had joked with Steph that she might now beat me to the goal of competing in a triathlon.

'It's not about me this time. It's about my children.'

She raised her eyebrows. 'You have been busy. If I remember correctly, last time we spoke you didn't have any children.'

'I've got temporary custody of them. I'm applying through Family Court to be granted full custody. They've both been through a lot of trauma and they need some therapy. I was wondering if you could recommend a psychologist who's experienced in dealing with traumatised children. I'd prefer that to my choosing someone at random.'

'I saw your story on the TV news a few weeks ago. Such a tragic incident. Are these the two children who witnessed it?'

I nodded. Maria tapped her pen on the desk. 'I know of a couple of psychologists who might fit the bill. Perhaps you'd better tell me the full story from the beginning, so I know exactly what we're dealing with.'

I gave her a brief summary of my relationship with Frankie, and our plans to escape and start a new life. When two CIB detectives interviewed me in hospital, they told me that on the morning of the tragedy, Eddie had gone into the garden shed to get his fishing gear and found two children's backpacks full of toys and clothes hidden behind a large crate of tools that he never used. He'd then threatened Frankie by gunpoint to divulge her plans, forcing her to send me the message and to meet me at the shopping centre as planned in order to trap me. His plan was indeed to execute me in front of Frankie 'to teach that cheatin' bitch a lesson.'

'I told Frankie not to pack anything; we could buy stuff when we got there. But I'm guessing she wanted the kids to have some of their things from home to make them feel more secure; and I'm also guessing that Eddie hardly ever set foot in the garden shed, so she felt safe hiding them there. It was just so unlucky he chose that day to go in there.'

If he hadn't, Frankie and I, and Jake and Aimee would probably be living in Gosford right now. A cosy cottage with a big back lawn for the kids to play on. And a white picket fence. I would have traipsed all over the city till I found one.

I was holding it together quite well until I came to the bit where Frankie started the car and headed straight for Eddie.

'I took off – it was my only chance. He was too quick – another couple of seconds and she would have run him down. He shot her, killed her instantly.'

The last memory I had of Frankie as she ploughed the car towards Eddie had replayed itself constantly in my mind over the last six months. 'Jake and Aimee...' A sob rose in my chest. I took a deep breath and quelled it. "No kid should have to go through that. The police told me later they found the kids still in the car. Jake was lying across Frankie's body, sobbing; and Aimee was curled up on the back seat with her thumb in her mouth – she'd cried herself to sleep.'

'Those poor children,' Maria said softly. 'I presume their father is in prison?'

'He's on remand for murder. He'll get life imprisonment; and by the time he gets out, Jake and Aimee will be adults.' I paused. 'There's something I haven't told you. Jake is my son. Frankie was pretty certain of it and I've since proved it through DNA testing. I haven't told him yet – he's got enough to deal with at the moment.'

Maria shook her head in amazement. 'You've all got more than enough to deal with. Your relationship with Frankie does explain a lot about your mental state when I last saw you. I knew there was something you were holding back.' She studied me. 'So how are things between you and Sarah?'

'Chilly. I'd arranged to meet her for coffee when I got the call from Frankie, so I'd stood her up. She was understandably very annoyed; although after she saw the report on the news that night, she apologised for sending me an abusive text message. Which, under the circumstances, I thought was pretty generous.'

The incident had been headline news that night and in the next day's newspapers. My father still hadn't forgiven me for dragging the family name into the mud of the murky criminal underworld. Nick and his family had been holidaying in London after his conference. They caught the next plane home and visited me in hospital. Recently, Nick had offered to pay for the children to attend a private school. I refused his offer, knowing it was made in good faith, assuring him I would be more than happy to send them to a public school.

My mother's maternal instincts towards Jake and Aimee had overridden any fear of social ostracism. She and Steph had been a great help with the practical, everyday things such as buying clothes and toys, as well as moral support to endure the nightmares that happened almost every night. My

own I could cope with, but when Jake or Aimee (or both –
usually one set off the other) woke up screaming or sobbing,
my heart would break anew and they invariably ended up
snuggled up in my bed for the night. Who needed it more,
them or me, it was hard to say.

'So what are your feelings towards Eddie now?' Maria
asked.

I grinned. 'So you've turned this into a therapy session
after all.'

I considered her question. 'To tell you the truth, I'm too
exhausted to feel much at the moment. I could say I hate him
and I'll never forgive him for what he did to Frankie and the
kids, and that's true. But at the same time, I can't afford to
let that anger rule my life, because it will also then rule the
lives of Jake and Aimee. And this is probably not what you
want to hear, but knocking Eddie out gave me a great deal of
satisfaction.'

Maria smiled. 'Sometimes it can be the only solution. But
don't quote me; I'll deny I ever said it.'

'And you'll be pleased to know I've taken up the guitar
again. I'm written some more songs and I'm negotiating with
a local indie record producer to sign up to his label.'

'That's great news.' She scribbled something on a piece
of notepaper. 'Here's the number of a psychologist I think
you'll find will be excellent for Jake and Aimee.'

Chapter 32

A year later. 3 November 2014

The polished marble of the memorial plaque gleamed in the gentle morning sunlight. 'Francis Margaret Slater. 23 March 1981 - 3 November 2013. Died at the age of 32. You are always with us. Will, Jake and Aimee.'

A golden urn of ashes stood in the glassed-in alcove beneath it. Below it on a shelf sat Aimee's moth-eaten rabbit and Jake's favourite racing car – the two toys the children had chosen to put in there so that, as Jake put it, 'Mummy won't forget us now she's in heaven'.

At the base of the plaque was a fresh bunch of daffodils and a helium balloon on a weighted string that said 'Mummy'. I tried to make the memorial centre at the crematorium bright and cheerful, a place the children would enjoy coming to.

Aimee picked up the balloon. 'Can I have this?'

'No, it's Mummy's,' Jake answered.

Aimee immediately burst into tears.

'Cry baby,' Jake taunted her.

'That's enough, Jake,' I said. 'Aimee, you can play with the balloon while we're here. It can be your special toy to play with when we come and visit Mummy.'

'Where's my special toy?' Jake whined.

'You can share the balloon with Aimee.'

Negotiating with courts and debt collectors on behalf of financially distressed adults belonged to another lifetime long ago – negotiating with children was an entirely new frontier.

Jake kicked at a tuft of grass. 'I hate Daddy.'

'Why?' I knew why, but I also knew it was important to let him talk about it.

'Because he killed Mummy.'

I hugged him to me, but he pushed me away.

'Me too,' Aimee chimed in, waving the balloon around in the air. 'I hate Daddy too.'

She was Jake's echo as well as his devoted shadow.

'I'll always hate him. Forever and ever,' Jake said.

'Forever 'n' ever,' Aimee said.

When they were ready, I would tell them the whole story. That their mother and I had loved each other very much; that she was killed trying to save my life; and that I was Jake's real Dad, but I considered Aimee my real daughter too, and loved her just as much as Jake.

I picked up my guitar case from the ground beside me. 'Come on, kids, I'm going to play Mummy a song.'

I led them over to a nearby seat, slid my guitar out of its case, and after a couple of warm-up chords, launched into 'Just Today'.

You're so tough on the outside

But you're just a little girl wanting to hide

Your eyes tell a story of sorrow and pain

But darling when I see you again

There will be no past

Just today.

As I sang, I could hear Frankie singing with me; her voice as clear as the morning, in perfect harmony with mine.

Jake put his hands over his ears 'Stop! I don't like that song!'

Aimee put her hands over her ears as well, giggling.

I couldn't help smiling. 'Looks like I'm overruled. What song would you like to sing?'

'Wheels On The Bus!' Aimee piped up.

'It has to be something Mummy would like,' Jake said.

'What do you think she would like?' I said.

He gazed back at me. Big, brown eyes. So solemn. Making an important decision, weighing up the pros and cons. A ghost from my childhood. I shivered.

'Wheels On The Bus,' he pronounced.

Aimee gave a squeal of delight and clapped her hands.

'Are you ready?' I strummed the introductory phrase then we launched into it.

'The wheels on the bus go round and round, round and round, round and round.

The wheels on the bus go round and round, early in the morning.'

Our voices floated through the crisp air. An elderly couple ambling by smiled, and the Mummy balloon fluttered gently in the breeze.

THE END

ACKNOWLEDGMENTS

I have a number of people in my support crew to thank – my partner Aaron, for his love and help with all things formatting and technical, my family for their moral support, and my longstanding critique partner Pam Mariko for her constant and invaluable feedback.

I also thank my other beta readers Jill Moffatt and Katharine Haworth for their comments and feedback, as well as lawyer Michael Robinson for taking time out of his busy schedule to read and comment on the legalities.

Thank-you for buying An Affair With Danger. I hope you enjoyed it.

I would appreciate it very much if you would take a few minutes to leave an honest review on Amazon or whichever site you bought it from. Reviews help other readers to decide whether they will enjoy the book, as well as helping it to gain more visibility and ultimately, more sales.

Nothing is more rewarding for me than people reading and enjoying my books.

Get my e-book of four short crime stories On The Edge by becoming a subscriber to Storey-Lines.
Go to http://storey-lines.com for your free copy now

I would also love to connect with you on the following social media sites:

Facebook http://www.facebook.com/RobinStoreywriter
Twitter https://twitter.com/RobinStorey1
Pinterest http://pinterest.com/robinstorey
LinkedIn http://www.linkedin.com/in/robinstoreyauthor
Instagram https://instagram.com/robinstorey55/
YouTube
https://www.youtube.com/user/RobinStoreyAuthor
Smashwords author page:
https://www.smashwords.com/profile/view/RobinStorey
Goodreads
http://www.goodreads.com/author/show/7057008.Robin_Storey

Other Books by Robin Storey

For other books in the Noir Nights series and Robin's stand-alone novels, please visit Storey-Lines http://storey-lines.com or find Robin Storey on Amazon or IngramSpark.

E-books are available at all major e-book retailers.

ABOUT THE AUTHOR

Robin Storey is an indie author who lives on the picturesque Sunshine Coast in Queensland, Australia. She's a former freelance writer who is hooked on writing novels – it's the most challenging, but also the most satisfying thing she's done.

Robin is a certified book nerd and recharges her creative batteries by getting out into nature – hiking and chilling out at the beach.